PUBLICATIONS

OF

Eighteenth-Century

Russian Literature

EDITOR-IN-CHIEF

Henry M. Nebel, Jr., Northwestern University

EDITORIAL COMMITTEE

John Fizer, Rutgers University
Marvin Kantor, Northwestern University

Selected Prose
of N. M. Karamzin

SELECTED PROSE

OF

N · M · Karamzin

TRANSLATED AND
WITH AN INTRODUCTION
BY HENRY · M · NEBEL · JR

Northwestern University Press
EVANSTON · 1969

Frontispiece portrait of
Nikolai Mikhailovich Karamzin
by I. N. Kramskii
(Rumiantsev Museum, Moscow)

Henry M. Nebel, Jr., is Associate Professor
in the Russian Department, Northwestern University.

To Sue, Althea, and Keith,
with all my love

Contents

ix

Contents

Foreword

IN RECENT YEARS many important works of Russian literature have become accessible to the English-speaking world through translations. However, these published titles largely represent either topical contemporary literature or additions to the works of nineteenth-century masters. The vast and informative body of eighteenth-century Russian literature—on which so much of the nineteenth century is predicated—has been largely ignored by Western translators and scholars. This series attempts to remedy this neglect through a translation of some major works of the significant prose writers, poets, and dramatists of the eighteenth century.

Foreword

Since much of the literature and many of these authors are relatively unknown in the West, each volume contains a carefully documented introduction which places the work and the man in the broader context of Russian and European culture. The translated text has been annotated to provide further guidance for the general reader. In this manner, it is the editor's hope to throw some light upon that hitherto dark eighteenth-century laboratory, whose stylistic, thematic, and linguistic experiments contributed so substantially to the literary successes of the past century.

Translator's Note

Nikolai Mikhailovich Karamzin is generally acknowledged to be the master prose stylist of eighteenth-century Russian literature. I was very much influenced by this reputation initially but, during my work on the translation itself, came to the conclusion that the prose, excellent as it is, deserves its reputation only in comparison with Karamzin's contemporaries and predecessors. When successful, the style is suggestively allusive, a nice blend of fact and fancy; when it fails, it is fluffy, repetitive, and harshly simple. My object in the translation was to render this style and content as exactly as the syntax and semantics of English would allow. In this fashion, I have tried to capture Karamzin's successes as well as failures, hoping not to compound the problem by confusing one with the other.

The Russian text used for all stories (except "Julia") is *N. M. Karamzin, Izbrannye sochineniia* ("N. M. Karamzin, Selected Works"), (Moscow-Leningrad: Izdatel'stvo khudozhestvennaia literatura, 1964), Vols. I and II. P. N. Berkov, the editor of this text, tried to conform to Karamzin's original punctuation as far as the rules of contemporary Russian permitted. I, too, have attempted to retain this punctuation since it is so much a part of Karamzin's style. However, to conform to English rules of punctuation, some slight changes were made. The Russian text used for "Julia" is taken from *Sochineniia Karamzina* ("Works of Karamzin"), Moscow, 1803.

The Library of Congress transliteration system has been used. However, the diacritical marks have been omitted as well as the symbols for the hard and soft signs when they occur at the end of words in the text. These symbols have been retained in the footnotes. When the Russian equivalent of an English first name appears in the translated text, the English form is used, e.g., Iuliia = Julia; when it appears in the editorial footnotes and introductory material, it is transliterated according to the Library of Congress system. Russian surnames found frequently in English literature are rendered in the introduction and text through the most commonly used transliteration, e.g., Dostoevsky rather than Dostoevskii; in the footnotes, the Library of Congress system is used.

I would like to express my gratitude to Mrs. Xenia Youhn of the Russian Department of Northwestern University for her constant help in deciphering the many passages which puzzled me. I would also like to thank Miss Anne Huseman and Miss Christa Suttner for their preliminary translation of "The Island of Bornholm." The version as it appears in the text has been completely revised and is my responsibility.

Translator's Note

Finally, I would like to thank the Research Committee of Northwestern University for making funds available for the typing of this manuscript and the editors of Northwestern University Press for their assistance.

H. M. N., Jr.

Introduction

N. M. Karamzin

LIFE

THE NAME OF NIKOLAI MIKHAILOVICH KARAMZIN
(1766–1825) is indissolubly connected with the city of Moscow and its intellectual circles.[1] Here in the seventies he
received his early education; here in the eighties he served his
apprenticeship with the Moscow Masons; and it was here in
the nineties that he published in his own journals and almanacs his most important prose fiction, essays, and poetry. In a

---

1. For a more detailed treatment of Karamzin's life and literature,
see my book, *N. M. Karamzin, A Russian Sentimentalist* (The
Hague: Mouton & Co., 1967).

3

very demonstrable sense, he is one of the finest products of the cultural ferment and antinomies of Moscow intellectual life in the last quarter of the eighteenth century and, like Moscow itself, a symbol of the old and the new which were fused in stubborn hostility to the "city of Peter's making," St. Petersburg.

Permeated by an alien mood and frequently ruled by foreign nobility and even an alien empress, St. Petersburg, the official capital of "all the Russias," provoked distrust and suspicion in many Russian minds. Founded on the periphery of the empire early in the century, the city symbolized the turning of Russia outward, toward Europe, especially toward the France of Versailles, which in the soft afterglow of the Sun King's reign provided models for the buildings, gardens, and, indeed, the habits and decorum of the Russian court. Moscow, on the other hand, remained simply and unfeignedly Russian, the center of the Orthodox faith, the repository of miracle-working icons, the guardian of the old manners and habits, in opposition to the foreign and foppish ways of St. Petersburg.

In the last decades of the eighteenth century, this distrust and suspicion pervaded the social and cultural rivalry between the two cities. The Moscow nobility viewed St. Petersburg then in much the same way as the arch-conservative views Washington today: as a center of bureaucratic and autocratic power intent upon curtailing the individual's privileges and prerogatives. Faced by this hostility and disturbed by the old Muscovite ways, Catherine II responded in kind, poking fun in her writings at Muscovite superstition and ignorance and visiting Moscow only rarely.

Deserted to some extent by the administration and, at times, snubbed by the court, Moscow did not stagnate. Quite the contrary; in the latter decades of the century, a resurgence occurred in her economic, social, educational, and intellectual life. In "Poor Liza," Karamzin writes with pride of Moscow, where "heavy barges . . . ply their way from the most fertile lands of the Russian empire and provide greedy Moscow with grain." Indeed, the single most important factor in the city's persistent vitality was the continuing development and expansion of her economic life. Karamzin points out only one element, the population increase (1735: 138,792; 1792: 175,000), which underlay the "greed" for more produce and manufactured goods. He does not mention the traditional role of Moscow as intermediary, or middleman, between the agricultural and industrial sectors of the country. This role expanded significantly, especially after the opening up of the southeast areas of the empire in the 1730's and the abolition of domestic customhouses in 1753, which greatly facilitated trade. From distant parts of the nation, cattle, fish, wine, and grain moved more freely to and through Moscow, and toward the end of the century—the period described by Karamzin—over one thousand vessels docked annually to unload their produce in Moscow.

Commerce and industry are to a certain extent educational and democratizing forces. Different social classes are brought into daily contact, a rudimentary education is required, profit and loss are based ideally on economic training and acumen rather than on social prerogatives. The demographic increase in Moscow during the latter part of the century occurred largely in the peasant class; obviously, these people made up the labor force of the burgeoning industrial and commercial enterprises and, to a minor degree, assumed entrepreneurial responsibilities. The number of merchants and *raznochintsy* (non-noble functionaries of some education from the merchant, clerical, or peasant strata) remained fairly constant throughout the period, but their wealth and, perhaps, power are indicated by the fact that in the seventies they owned 55 to 60 per cent of all the houses in Moscow. In 1756, a special high school associated with the University of Moscow was established for their children, and in the eighties the enrollment of this school outnumbered that of the high school for children of the nobility.

The expanding economic activity and the incipient social awareness of the middle and lower classes had a salutary effect upon the intellectual life of Moscow. A more broadly based reading public, interested in pertinent economic, social, and cultural news, was being created from this melting pot. The number of journals and newspapers published in Moscow increased significantly. In the third quarter of the eighteenth century, there were only four publications, while in the decade 1779 to 1789 some ten literary journals and four scientific magazines were published by Nikolai I. Novikov (1744–1818), the most prominent figure in the Russian Enlightenment. His Moscow publications, written in an easy style and a conversational idiom, appealed to the lower and middle classes and kept them informed of the economic details of Moscow life as well as of its cultural events. I. I. Dmitriev (1760–1837), a close friend of Karamzin and a poet of the Russian pre-Romantic movement, noted the composition and growth of the reading public by observing in 1789 that not only "educated people but also merchants, soldiers, serfs, and even gingerbread and bread salesmen" read.

The rise of a more broadly based reading public in Moscow is less significant for our purposes than the class origin of the writers, poets, essayists, and journalists. The men chiefly responsible for the Russian Enlightenment—the Freemasons, university professors, and representatives of various cultural organizations—were drawn by and large from the nobility, a social group which found the climate of Moscow most salubrious. In her memoirs, Catherine the Great ruefully observes that "it is quite deserted in Petersburg. A large part of the well-to-do live here because of their obligations, not of their own desire. When the court returns from Moscow, almost all the courtiers take leave in order to remain there, some for a year, some for six months, some for a month or several weeks." [2] These dignitaries did indeed prefer Moscow. Far removed from the seat of autocratic power, the traditionally informal way of life and the cheaper cost of living appealed to them. However, not only the upper nobility was attracted to Moscow. Just as the English gentry descended upon London in the late autumn, so the provincial gentry from neighboring regions descended upon Moscow to stay until early spring. Of course, the city, the economic hub of their world, was the basic reason for the influx, but the provincial gentry also came to provide for the education of their children and to visit the theaters (where the bourgeois drama and *comédie larmoyante* were quite successful), operas, private concerts, and the English Club, which had opened in 1770. The gentry participated in a significant measure in the city's economic life, some merely as customers, some as entrepreneurs, and some, a small group, as administrators of industrial enterprises.

This economic and social ferment, cross-pollinating Moscow society, was the basis of the cultural renaissance that occurred in the last quarter of the century. At the center of the renaissance was an institution, the University of Moscow, and a social-cultural movement, the Moscow Freemasons. The young intellectuals who attended the institution and those who participated in the movement received a remarkably similar intellectual indoctrination. This should not be surprising, for the personnel of the University of Moscow and the Moscow Masonic movement were closely intertwined; e.g., M. N. Kheraskov (1733–1807) and I. I. Melissino (?–?), curators, were prominent Masons, and Johann G. Schwartz

---

2. *Zapiski Ekateriny II* ("Memoirs of Catherine II") (St. Petersburg: n.p., 1906), p. 85.

Introduction

(1751–1784), a professor of German, was the Masonic leader in the early eighties. More important, many leading intellectuals of both the institution and the movement were favorably disposed to a new literary taste, transmitted immediately from Germany but originating in England. Many university professors, Germanophile Russians or Germans, introduced their students to contemporary German philosophy, aesthetics, and literature. Similarly, the Moscow Masons were influenced by German Masonic ideas, which they zealously propagated in their publications and actions.

The doors of the University of Moscow were opened in January, 1755, to meet the need for teachers, doctors, and civil functionaries. Influenced by the German university system, the lecture courses were large, conducted in Latin (until 1767, when Russian was introduced), and highly theoretical and abstract. In a period when Russia needed a well-developed system of secondary schools, an institution of higher education was established. Perhaps as a counterbalance to the impractical idealism of the abstruse formal curriculum, many societies formed, dissolved, and regrouped in or about the university in the seventies and eighties. They differed in their subjects of interest, ranging from history (Free Russian Society) and translations (Translating Seminar) to pedagogy (Pedagogical Seminar) and belles-lettres (Assembly of University Nurslings), but were unified by the practical and pragmatic training they provided for the future historian, translator, teacher, poet, and journalist.

The Masonic philosophy was a most significant factor in the drift toward mysticism, occultism, and obscurantism which marked Moscow intellectual life in the late seventies and eighties. Earlier, the Russian Masonic movement had been strongly influenced by the deistic philosophy and political liberalism of English Freemasonry. These early Masons espoused the cult of reason, rational morality, and a natural religion opposed to that of revelation and miracle. However, in the seventies, the spirit of rationalism seems to have been cast out by the devil of philosophical shallowness, cynicism, atheism, and a self-serving ostentation. Novikov moved from St. Petersburg to Moscow in 1779, dramatically divorcing himself from the influence which he described as "Voltairean," understanding it to mean skepticism, atheism, and immorality.[3]

This disillusionment with reason and rationality was a reflection of contemporary European Masonic developments. The Rosicrucian order, which gained prominence in the seventies in Germany, reflected the new, more mystical, orientation in many respects. Its brethren were interested in magic, alchemy, mystical cures for illnesses, theosophy, and cabalism; they preferred seeking truth through occult practices and magical knowledge rather than through moral perfection. In 1781, Johann G. Schwartz was sent abroad to study German pedagogical methods; in Berlin, he received the acts for a Rosicrucian order, which he established in Moscow upon his return.

In 1782, Schwartz defined the new system, in a conversation with Novikov, as the "cognition of God, nature, and man by the shortest and truest path."[4] Unfortunately, the route twisted and turned excruciatingly and caused the Moscow Masons great difficulties. The "shortest and truest path" to

3. This interpretation of Voltaire overlooks the fact that he was a deist, a believer in God if not in providence, and an impudent skeptic who was always guided by a prudent common sense. Voltaire was known in Russia primarily through his *Lettres Philosophiques* (1734), whose irreverent satire of the clergy and religion helps explain this Russian view of the great Frenchman.

4. As quoted by V. Bogoliubov, *N. I. Novikov i ego vremia* ("N. I. Novikov and His Time"), (Moscow: M. & S. Sabashnikov, 1916), p. 259.

God was essentially that of divine revelation, which was allowed the morally perfect man, and, needless to say, only members of the order could achieve this grace. This doctrine of divine revelation—mystical in concept, promising contact between man and God—could and did lead to many abuses. Occasionally, one of the brethren in the ecstasy of communion would glimpse not God but the Devil. The path to a "cognition of . . . nature" led to even greater difficulties. The Moscow Masons turned to the knowledge of the Middle Ages, alchemy and magic, to fathom nature's secrets. In further pursuit of such knowledge, they dispatched several members to Germany for training in alchemy and a field closely allied with it at that time, chemistry.

The Masons were always eager to proselytize young intellectuals, and, despite the mysticism and occultism, they provided eminently practical training in translating, writing, and journalism for their young associates. Many of the university groups had been organized, financed, and directed by the Masons for a very practical reason: to train editors, translators, and journalists to carry out their varied work. When Novikov assumed control of the Moscow University Printing House in 1779, he changed his place of residence but not his lifelong dream, which was defined by one scholar as "the difficult task of propagating reading and education among the middle class, of awakening everywhere a quick consciousness of enlightenment as the source of firm moral principles." [5] Young Russians were recruited to participate in these truly enormous labors. In the first three years of Novikov's management, the Printing House published and sold more books than in its entire previous twenty-five years of existence. Supplied with trained or partially trained young men from these societies and

5. N. S. Tikhonravov, "Novikov," *Sochineniia* ("Works"), (Moscow: M. & S. Sabashnikov, 1898), III, 131.

the university, Novikov proceeded to publish a series of magazines and almost 900 books—which made up approximately one-third of all the titles published in Russia in this decade—and to open bookstores in Moscow, Poltava, Simbirsk, Tambov, and other Russian cities.

Karamzin's most creative days were spent in Moscow, but it was not his birthplace. He was born December 1, 1766, the second of four children, in the small village of Mikhailovka, in the middle regions of the Volga, and raised in Simbirsk (now Ulyanovsk, celebrated as the birthplace of Lenin), some four hundred miles southeast of the "city of the golden cupolas." Mikhail Egorovich, Karamzin's father and a retired army captain, exemplified many facets of the cultural revolution fostered by Peter the Great, especially its veneration of the West and Western educational methods. Consequently, as a child Nikolai Mikhailovich was tutored in German, allowed to read Russian translations of French romances, and, when old enough, attended first a pension in Simbirsk and then, in 1777, one in Moscow.

The latter pension was supervised by a university professor of rhetoric, poetry, and mythology, Johannes Matthias Schaden, and was typical of the many private boarding schools which flourished in Moscow in the seventies and eighties. Training schools for the nobility, their purpose was to prepare the student for entrance into the university or, failing that, to help him assume his responsibilities as a noble in society. In this pension, Karamzin continued his sentimental education which had begun, in childhood, with the reading of French *romans d'aventure,* an education that fitted in well with the rising tide of sensibility. Schaden used the fables and lectures of the German moralist, Christian Fürchtegott Gellert, to develop in his young pupils their intuitive moral sense and to attack the prevailing rationalism and materialism. In Schaden's pension, Karamzin continued his study of German, began to study French, and was introduced to English literature in translation. During his last year, in 1781, he also attended lectures at the University of Moscow.

Karamzin had been enrolled at birth in the elite Preobrazhenskii regiment by his father, and upon finishing his studies he was called to active duty in St. Petersburg. Here he renewed an acquaintance with a compatriot from Simbirsk, I. I. Dmitriev, who was also in service in St. Petersburg. Their similar origin, their enthusiasm for literature, and the loneliness they must have felt in the large, somewhat alien city threw them together and they became inseparable friends. Later Karamzin was to become Dmitriev's literary guide, but at the outset of this friendship Dmitriev provided the spark and inspiration. Dmitriev knew and loved French and Russian literature, especially the light verse of men such as Dorat and Parny in France and Sumarokov and Murav'ev in Russia; he had already published several translations. Karamzin had been introduced to German literature in Schaden's pension, but his command and knowledge of French literature was weak. Dmitriev acquainted Karamzin with this literature, and Karamzin, inspired by his friend's publications, soon translated a poem from the German.[6]

Military service was not of long duration, nor was it crowned by spectacular achievement. With his father's death in 1784, Karamzin retired from the service and returned to his Simbirsk estate. The ensuing twelve months were most important for Karamzin, for he came to realize that the aimless existence of a provincial landlord—balls, card games, social gatherings—was not the fulfillment of those ideals he had absorbed in Schaden's pension or of the dedication to literature he had witnessed in Dmitriev. Karamzin seemed well on his way to becoming another faceless member of the petty gentry

6. Gessner's "Das holzerne Bein."

when, in his own words, a "beneficent Providence" saved him
from "ultimate destruction." [7] In less grandiloquent words,
Karamzin met and deeply impressed Ivan Petrovich Turgenev,
a prominent Mason and intellectual. A successful Simbirsk
merchant and a friend of Novikov and Schwartz, Turgenev
was active in the manifold ventures of the Moscow Masons
and an eager recruiter of young Russians to the cause. Turgenev urged the young man to go west, to Moscow, and be of
service there to humanity. Turgenev struck a responsive chord
for, in 1785, Karamzin dutifully moved to Moscow, settled
down in an old stone house near the Menshikov Tower of the
Friendly Learned Society (founded by the Masons in 1782 for
the continuing intellectual training of their young associates),
and began a period of literary and journalistic study under
Masonic guidance.

The next four years were to be the most significant educative years of Karamzin's life. He eventually withdrew from
the Masonic circle in 1789, but not before the brethren had
stabilized his intellectual interests and set the course of his
future intellectual development.

Since Karamzin had some slight experience as a translator
of German, he began his activities in the Friendly Learned
Society in this capacity, translating a religiously mystical poem
from the German in 1786.[8] Such a translation was typical of
Novikov's publishing activities: He worked to expand the
Russian Enlightenment along Christian moral principles and,
consequently, published many didactic moral and religious
tracts. Karamzin's initial translations were in this vein, but his
later efforts differed on aesthetic as well as moral grounds. He

7. *Perepiska Karamzina c Lafaterom* ("Correspondence of
Karamzin with Lavater"), (St. Petersburg: Akademiia Nauk, 1894),
p. 6.
8. "Über den Ursprung des Übels," by Albrecht von Haller
(1708–1777).

avoided moralizing pieces in favor of an appealing, well-wrought tale, play, or poem. It might be that he simply rejected the didacticism that marked Masonic literature in the eighties and reverted to Novikov's earlier ideal: to create a literature that would amuse as well as edify. Or, perhaps, the childhood reading of romances, the pension experience with Gellert's delightful moralizing, the adolescent acceptance of light verse, made Karamzin very aware that literature could be delightful and still not demoralizing.

Even while the young Mason was translating these poems, he was busy with something dearer to his heart, a translation of Shakespeare's *Julius Caesar*. This play had attracted much attention in the eighteenth century from translators and adaptors, for its picture of corruptive tyranny and its flagrantly successful disregard of classical aesthetic rules appealed both to the opponents of political absolutism and the exponents of pre-Romanticism. It is this latter aspect that Karamzin singles out in his Preface, the first critical defense in Russia of Shakespeare's violation of such "rules," by pointing out the wide emotional range of the characters, the bard's inventiveness, variety, and, most of all, his imagination, "which would not be bound by any prescriptions." A year later, in 1788, he published his translation of Lessing's bourgeois drama, *Emilia Galotti*, a complex study of a virtuous family's destruction through the machinations of Prince Gonzaga, a courtier who is intent upon satisfying his most vicious passions. The translation is a defense of a more modern theater and an attack upon the classical drama, where exalted beings from antiquity play out their fates according to the orthodoxies of time, place, and unity.

These two translations suggest the distant pole toward which Karamzin had boldly moved in his own literary education. After his undisciplined literary activity in St. Petersburg, Karamzin found himself in a group dominated by definite literary tastes originating in the pre-Romantic literature of Germany, England, and France. The developing pre-Romantic tendencies can be discerned in the various magazines published under the general editorship of Novikov and Schwartz,[9] who drew heavily upon the eighteenth-century literature of sensibility for their translations and adaptations. Translations of Young, Gessner, Gellert, Thomson, Rousseau, praises of Sterne and Jacobi, and references to Wieland, Milton, and Shakespeare appeared on their pages. However disparate this literature, it was unified by several themes: the interest in man's subjective world, the mysterious rapport between man and nature, the tortuous joys of melancholy, solitude, the delight in enthusiasm and inspiration, the simple life—all of which were to act as a thematic magnet for Karamzin and to be polarized in the cult of sensibility that he fostered in his poetry and prose.

Aleksander A. Petrov, a young Mason with whom Karamzin shared an apartment in the house of the Friendly Learned Society, was the most direct contact for many of these pre-Romantic ideas. Petrov had attended a course of lectures given by Schwartz in which the aesthetic theories of Aristotle, Cicero, Horace, Boileau, Batteux, and Baumgarten were analyzed. Petrov became seriously interested in aesthetic problems and transmitted this interest to his young roommate. He also encouraged Karamzin to study English literature more systematically, corrected his translations and original work sympathetically, and in general helped channel the vague idealism and rambling interests of his young friend into a definite aesthetic direction.

In 1785, Novikov began a new journal, *Readings for Chil-*

9. The more important journals were *Utrenii Svet* ("Morning Light"), 1777–1780; *Moskovskoe Ezhemesiachnoe Izdanie* ("Moscow Monthly Publication"), 1781; and *Vecherniaia Zaria* ("Evening Light"), 1782.

dren for Their Hearts and Minds ("Detskoe chtenie dlia serdtsa i razuma"), destined for the young reader and, consequently, containing articles on natural history, history, and morality, all enlivened by profuse quotations from the Bible. In 1787, Petrov and Karamzin assumed editorial responsibility for the journal and changed its contents considerably. The historical articles disappeared, biblical quotations were shortened, and only two moral tales were published. The emphasis was now placed primarily on literary and artistic pieces. This magazine was Karamzin's real laboratory, and Petrov was his constant guide. Readings for children had to be instructive, educative, interesting, and short. Karamzin's first sustained venture, quite different in tone, if not in ultimate didactic purpose, from his initial Masonic contribution, was his translation in 1787 and 1788 of Madame de Genlis' moral tales from *Les Veillées du Château* and *Nouveaux contes moraux et nouvelles historiques.* He also published excerpts from his translation of Thomson's *The Seasons,* some original poetry, and two prose pieces, "A Stroll" and "Eugene and Julia."

Already in a letter of May, 1785, Petrov noted the ease with which Karamzin was successfully assimilating the literary knowledge of the Masonic circle. In 1789, Karamzin had mastered this material and could go no further: He had received intensive training in editorial and journalistic work, had gained valuable insights in translating, and, most important of all, had read widely in the Russian and European prose and poetry of sensibility, from which he derived the techniques, themes, and the "language of the heart" to be applied in his own creations of the nineties. A predilection for the new bourgeois drama and for dramatists who probe "human nature deeply," a delight in descriptive poetry, a willingness to recount his own personal experience, and a realization that literature to be successful must be attractive—these were all part of his literary inheritance from the Masons. But Karamzin had exhausted this experience and turned now toward the unlimited vistas of Europe. In May, 1789, in his twenty-second year, the young Muscovite began a journey which took him to the capitals of Europe and to England, to the great (and the near great) men-of-letters, Herder, Kant, Wieland, Weisse, Bonnet, and Lavater. He recounted his reactions to those sights and personalities in his major prose work, *The Letters of a Russian Traveler* ("Pis'ma russkogo puteshestven-nika"), published in his journals of the nineties.[10]

The Masonic period of Karamzin's apprenticeship coincided with a period of sharp hostility between St. Petersburg and Moscow. The passive cultural competition threatened to break out into open political conflict. These events are closely tied to the foreign liaisons, putative and real, of the Moscow Masons. Schwartz, in his trip to Berlin in 1781, had contacted several Rosicrucians who were members of the entourage of the future King of Prussia, Frederick William II. In 1787, Russia's relations with Prussia had deteriorated and Catherine was suspicious of any group which maintained relations, however tenuous, with the Prussian government. In this same year the Moscow Masons approached the Grand Duke Paul, Catherine's son, and sought to convert him to their order. In so doing, they blundered magnificently. Catherine had long distrusted the Masons, resenting their usurpation of rights she considered to belong to the state, e.g., educational and philanthropic activity, and she now feared that a movement was afoot to place Paul on the throne with the help of the Masons and their Prussian allies. She began to harass the order, increasing the censorship of their publications and persecuting the Masons themselves. Finally, in 1791, Catherine forced

10. Portions were published in the *Moskovskii Zhurnal* ("Moscow Journal"), 1791–92, and in *Aglaia,* 1794–95. The first separate edition, expurgated by the censor, was published in 1797. The first complete edition appeared in 1801.

Introduction

Novikov to close his publishing house and, in the spring of 1792, had him arrested.

In the dangerous atmosphere of government suspicion and distrust which existed at the end of the eighties, Karamzin's Masonic period came to an end. He attributed this parting to the excessive mysticism and the absurd ritualism of the circle, all of which hindered the dispassionate search for the truth. This explanation is consistent with Karamzin's intellectual maturation during these years and should suffice. The Masons contributed a great deal to Karamzin's intellectual growth, but he never accepted their narrow religious-mystical orientation wholeheartedly. Karamzin was a writer rather than a preacher, and such an orientation only served to interfere with the pursuit of his own aesthetic interests.

Upon his return from England in September, 1790, he began his literary labors in earnest. While Karamzin is one of the most important writers of the turn of the century, it must not be forgotten that he also was one of the most important publishers. Starting with his first independent venture, the *Moscow Journal* ("Moskovskii Zhurnal") (1791–92), continuing through his almanacs *Aglaia* (Book I, 1794; Book II, 1795) and *Aonides* (Book I, 1796; Book II, 1797), and culminating in his *Herald of Europe* ("Vestnik Evropy") (1801 to 1803, when he relinquished the editorship), Karamzin worked indefatigably to attract and expand the reading public, to introduce and exemplify new literary genres, and to fashion a literary language and create a literary style for succeeding generations. His literature has the merits and the defects of this periodical format: His stories are often short and highly imitative; they are written in an attractive if somewhat fluffy prose; his poetry is often light, consisting largely of love lyrics, personal lyrics, and anacreontic verse; his articles make a few simple points, simply. Any criticism of the shallowness, ephemeral quality, and lack of sustained probing in Karamzin's art must recognize the limits in direction and depth forced upon him by the pressures of meeting deadlines, rounding up material, and the profit-and-loss factors.

With this in mind, Karamzin's contributions to Russian literature still remain significant and pervasive. He did not introduce sentimentalism into Russia, but he was the first to exemplify its main tenets in a sustained and coherent fashion. His most famous tales, "Poor Liza" and "Natalie, the Boyar's Daughter," appeared in the *Moscow Journal* in 1792 and the later tale, "The Island of Bornholm," written in 1793, appeared in *Aglaia* in 1794. "Julia," originally destined for *Aglaia* in 1794, was not published until 1796. Despite their variety, a definite uniformity in theme, characterization, and method of treatment runs through these tales. Love is the passion most frequently treated; it is an etherealized emotion, seemingly touched by a divine power. His characters, drawn largely from the middle classes of the nobility, are typical *belles âmes* of the eighteenth century. They are deeply sensitive, given to tears, beneficence, and virtue. Finally, Karamzin attempts to create the impression of verisimilitude to impress upon his readers the truth—and its relevance—of the tale. The article "What Does the Writer Need?" was published in *Aglaia* in 1794 and is a good, if somewhat brief, explanation of two important facets of sentimental art, its intensely subjective nature and strong moral imperative. The last article selected for translation from Karamzin's work of the nineties, the "Preface" to the second book of *Aonides,* appeared in 1797 and provided the aesthetic rationalization for his poetry; in its emphasis on the personal world of the poet, it is similar in theme to the other article.

Despite this probing of his own subjective world, Karamzin is not an "original" in Edward Young's sense of those "who extend the republic of letters and add a new province to its dominion," but he did "extend the republic" of Russian letters by artful imitation and adaptation. He was the first to translate Laurence Sterne from the original English and the first to use many Sternean techniques in Russian prose. The spoof of reality, the digression, the indecent chasteness of the narrator, the language of glances, tones, and manners, and the visual clarity of the poses all find their way into his prose, most apparently in "Natalie, the Boyar's Daughter." Similarly, Karamzin had translated J. F. Marmontel's *Contes moraux*, 1761, for the *Moscow Journal* and then proceeded to write his own moral tale, "Julia," based upon "L'Heureux Divorce," one of the Frenchman's most charming stories. He makes use of the same moral, the same characters, and the same incidents to portray the vagaries of romantic love. Finally, "The Island of Bornholm" and "Natalie, the Boyar's Daughter" make obvious use of certain themes and descriptive techniques borrowed from Macpherson's Ossianic poems, portions of which Karamzin had translated for the *Moscow Journal*. While these tales are often imitative and derivative, they broke the ground for an entire new period in Russian literature and, in their own way, can be called creative, if not "original."

The last years of Catherine's reign were gloomy and difficult for Karamzin. Petrov, his intellectual guide and friend, died in 1793, and Karamzin's "eternal grief" took long to pass. Many of his Masonic friends had suffered grievously at Catherine's hands,[11] and Karamzin himself was suspected of traveling to Europe for some subversive reason. The empress, however, had no conclusive evidence that might be used to punish the young editor and journalist; on the other hand, she acquiesced in the order that his translation of *Julius Caesar,* along with several of Novikov's publications, be burned as

11. Novikov had been imprisoned in Schlüsselberg Fortress; A. M. Kutuzov and I. V. Lopukhin, both intimate friends, had been exiled.

"pernicious." In the spring of 1793, Karamzin moved to his country estate near Simbirsk and for the next several years lived there or on the estate near Moscow of a dear friend, Anastasia Pleshcheeva, whom he had met in the spring days of his Moscow period. She was his intellectual consort and guide, the "dear friend of his heart" who provided the quiet atmosphere and necessary seclusion which allowed him to work during these trying years.

It was a period of persecution, whether real or imagined. Karamzin's withdrawal gave rise to rumors that he was dead or exiled. Perhaps government suspicion of the Masons, which continued to linger, prompted these rumors. Perhaps the conduct of Catherine, not openly hostile but cold and aloof toward him, one of the foremost Russian men-of-letters of the time, set tongues wagging. The obscurantist repression that followed in Russia after the French Revolution challenged the small gains made by Novikov and his associates. Deep in the countryside, Karamzin still managed to continue the struggle which had been undertaken by the Masons. In a series of articles written for *Aglaia,* he came to the defense of learning, science, and art and attempted to refute the claims of those "misosophists" who attributed all the world's ills to the Enlightenment.

Catherine died in the autumn of 1796, and Paul ascended the throne. Paul had been sympathetic to the Masons, and Karamzin looked to the release of his old associates and an improvement in the political and cultural climate. Paul's irrational acts quickly dispelled Karamzin's hopes. Paul seemed more intent upon discrediting Catherine's actions than upon establishing a rational and wise rule. The atmosphere was still as baleful and threatening as it had been during the last years of Catherine's regime, and Karamzin, conscious of this, did not undertake any new or bold ventures, but rather confined himself to a republication of material printed earlier.

Introduction

Alexander I ascended the throne in the winter of 1801, and there was a promise of a more liberal era. The new tsar issued more tolerant instructions to the censor which allowed "reasonable and modest research for truth," tolerated more contacts with foreigners, which had been prohibited by Paul, and permitted the opening of printing houses which had been closed by Paul. In this promising atmosphere Karamzin began his last journal, *Herald of Europe,* which differed markedly from his previous ventures. In the politically repressive atmosphere of Catherine's last years, Karamzin confined his interests to literature, art, and drama. In the bright dawn of Alexander's era, he ventured to discuss not only literary and social but political problems as well on the pages of his journal. The first section of the *Herald of Europe* was devoted to the contemporary European political and cultural scene. In translations and original articles, Karamzin presented to his Russian readers Bonaparte and Pitt, the Austrian coalition, and the ramifications of French relations; he helped make the foreign familiar. Our selections from this journal are drawn from the second section, which was primarily a moralistic critique of Russian society. "On the Book Trade and Love of Reading in Russia," 1802, praises Novikov's contributions to the Russian Enlightenment, while the article, "Why Is There So Little Writing Talent in Russia?", 1802, comments on the social and literary difficulties the Russian creative artist faced at the turn of the century. The other two essays, "My Confession," 1802, and "The Emotional and the Cold: Two Characters," 1803, elaborate upon the rational, unemotional man-of-action—not without a certain covert admiration on Karamzin's part—and represent a decided moderation of his previous sentimental views.

These early years of the nineteenth century were years of happy, fruitful endeavor. However, they were not unmixed with sorrow. Karamzin had married Elisabeth Ivanovna Protasova, the youngest sister of Anastasia Pleshcheeva, in 1801 and an idyllic year of happiness followed. Soon it was discovered that his wife was suffering from a serious illness, perhaps tuberculosis, and she died in the spring of 1802. Bereft, the grieving husband found consolation in his work and in the elaboration of a new venture, the writing of a history of the Russian state, from its origins to the contemporary period.

In September, 1803, Karamzin wrote to a close friend, Murav'ev, a former tutor to the tsar and an assistant minister of education, requesting a government stipend "to write a History, neither vulgar nor shameful." Murav'ev evidently pleaded successfully, for in about a month a ukase was published in Alexander's name granting Karamzin an annual stipend of 2,000 rubles to write a "complete history of our Fatherland." The remaining years of Karamzin's life were devoted to this enormous project: These are years of constant research, of hobnobbing with the court, of quarrels with Speranskii, the tsar's state secretary and close adviser, and with Alexander himself (which followed upon his reading Karamzin's work, "Memoir on Ancient and Modern Russia" ("Zapiska o drevnei i novoi Rosii")—largely an attack upon Speranskii's projected governmental reforms—years of dislocation caused by the Napoleonic conflict and the necessary move to St. Petersburg in 1816 in order to supervise the publication of the history. By 1803, Karamzin had concluded his career as poet, writer of tales and essays, and editor; his remaining years were dedicated to his twelve-volume work, *A History of the Russian State* ("Istoriia rossiiskogo gosudarstva").

The emperor greeted him warmly when he was presented on March 15, 1816, at the St. Petersburg court and agreed to print the first eight volumes of the history in the military printing house. Karamzin transported his family there in the spring (he had remarried in 1804), hoping to remain about two years to guide his volumes through the press and then to return to Moscow. But he was possessed by a strange premonition in the summer that he would die in Petersburg without ever returning to his "quiet Moscow." This premonition proved true. He stayed on for some ten years, a reluctant celebrity invited to court functions and an eager editor working incessantly on his history; but he never again returned to Moscow. He railed against St. Petersburg, its onerous social obligations, and swore, "I shall never leave my bones here." Fate decreed otherwise. After a short illness he died on May 22, 1826, and was buried in the Nevskoe Cemetery. A marble slab decorated with a laurel wreath bears the simple inscription, "Karamzin."

WRITINGS

VISSARION BELINSKII, the furious and indefatigable gadfly of Russian literary developments, found much of eighteenth-century literature insufferably petty, but he grudgingly admitted the potency of Karamzin's influence and dubbed an entire epoch, 1790–1820, the "Karamzin Period." That this might not be understood as praise, the Russian critic censures Karamzin's "childish" stories and, in general, strips his contributions of any permanent value. From his vantage point in some Schellingean empyrean, Belinskii also cast aspersions on the tendentiousness of Karamzin, querying whether "the vocation of an artist can lend itself to a premeditated aim, no matter how splendid that aim might be?" The answer of this critic, who was later to praise Gogol's satire for this very premeditation, is an obvious, although unstated, "Undoubtedly not!"

Let us be charitable and accept the idea that Karamzin was a "premeditated" artist, one who dealt with the specific social

24

and literary problems of his time and from a specific point of view. Art is not born only of art, in Malraux's concept, but significant art, like a rebellion, rises from a complex interaction of the man, society, and the medium of expression. Premeditation is an obvious necessity, for it implies a coherent comment on society in whatever medium the artist chooses. It is this premeditation that gives unity to Karamzin's contribution to Russian literature; this coherence of philosophical outlook and aesthetic attitude makes the artist significant, if not great, and explains his impact upon his own and later literary generations.

The articles and stories of this edition have been selected to indicate the artist's resolutions of social and cultural problems through the medium of his art. In the article, "On the Book Trade and Love of Reading in Russia," Karamzin clearly defines the two main cultural problems facing the writer in the last decades of the eighteenth century: First and most important was the lack of a broad interest in literature, in all reading in general, on the part of the Russian public; and, second, was the need for literature, if it was to appeal to a semi-literate people, to be enjoyable.

It was Novikov who saw the distant horizon and crossed the immediate bogs of apathy and ignorance toward the future. Editor, publisher, bookseller, Novikov tried in manifold ways to expand the reading public, varying the subject matter of his newspapers and journals to include articles on local and foreign political events, educational and social material, commercial and economic information. In so doing, he attracted readers not only from the nobility but from the lesser nobility, and merchants and burghers as well.

As the venerative mood of "On the Book Trade" suggests, Karamzin deeply admired Novikov, believed in his methods, and felt that in this area he was continuing his master's work. His own publications of the nineties, the *Moscow Journal,*

Aglaia, Aonides, were deliberately written to appeal to the middle levels of the nobility, to amuse, inform, educate, and satisfy the tastes of a people who were just becoming conscious of the salutary effect literature might have on their private lives. To this end, the *Moscow Journal* contained educative, light reading, reviews of plays, original Russian poetry and prose, translations from the German, English, and French, anything but "theological, mystical, excessively scholarly, pedantic, dry pieces," as Karamzin informs us in his initial announcement of the journal's publication.

The second point of this article concerns Russian literary development and reveals Karamzin's own aesthetic standard, which, somewhat modified, is central to his literary creativity. Since the likes and dislikes of the reading public indicate the popularity of a particular type of literature, Karamzin rhetorically asks, "What type of book is sold most among us?" And his answer, based on personal inquiries, is "Novels!" The reason for this popularity is obvious: This genre pictures "the world and people, who are similar to us, in interesting situations, depicting the most powerful and at the same time the most common passion in its varied activities." The "common passion," love, is the subject of the older adventure novels, which from the fifties were available to many Russians either in translation or in the original, and of the so-called "English novel," which had slowly gained in popularity during the last third of the century. Richardson in England, Rousseau in France, and Goethe in Germany were its most successful exponents. Their characters, drawn from the lower classes (*Pamela*) or the lower levels of the nobility (Werther or St. Preux), are complicated emotional beings, whose sensitivity and complexity are revealed through the authors' analysis of their situational entanglements.

"We have more translated than original works and, consequently," as Karamzin justly observes, "foreign authors have gained fame among the Russians." In the last decades of the century, the names of Richardson, Fielding, and Sterne became familiar to many Russians, largely through translations from the French. The tradition of the "English novel" was also sustained in the many French and German imitations which found their way into Russia. Apart from Rousseau and Goethe, who were available in the original, other practitioners of this literary trend who proved extremely popular among the Russians were Baculard d'Arnold, Mme. de Genlis, Florian, Meissner, and Marmontel.

The accessibility and success of "foreign authors" in Russia made the Russians a bit hesitant to try their hand at this genre. In 1766, Fedor Emin wrote *The Letters of Ernest and Doravra* in strict imitation of Rousseau. The hero, Ernest, a member of the lesser nobility, follows the dictates of his own emotions only to come into conflict with the hypocritical upper nobility and to be frustrated eventually in his love for Doravra. In 1789 Emin's son, Nikolai, wrote *Game of Fate,* whose violent and impetuous hero plays the game of life according to Werther and is led by his passions into open hostility toward society and morality. Finally, in the same year, Pavel L'vov wrote a tale of the attempted seduction of a virtuous peasant girl by a profligate nobleman, which, as the title, *A Russian Pamela,* suggests, follows the winding and often windy path of Richardson's novel.

This in brief was the Russian prose scene when Karamzin began his journalistic career. In 1787–88 Karamzin had translated some fifteen *Contes moraux* of the very popular Frenchwoman, Madame de Genlis, and this exercise had a strong influence on his own narrative art. Thematically, Madame de Genlis eliminated the sequential intrigues of the *roman d'aventure,* concentrating instead on simple situations and a single passion. The mood of intimacy, the frank, sometimes stern, revelation of these tales arise from the initial supposi-

Introduction

tion: Madame de Clemire narrates these tales to her three young children for their recreation and moral edification. Since this is a family group, the narrator frequently interposes herself to interpret an event, to respond to a child's question, or to philosophize upon the action. These interpretations, responses, and philosophy are morally edifying and are more important than the story itself, which usually is a description of one or two characters, drawn from the lower classes or middle nobility, and of a moral crisis in their lives.

The purpose of such tales, to amuse and to educate; the setting, ordinary domestic situations; and the narrative techniques, where the author's personality is a vital element of the exposition, appear in Karamzin's tales and simply imitate what had been taking place in European and English prose in the previous half century. Because of the restrictions placed upon him by the format of *Readings for Children*, Karamzin selected this genre as his métier and proceeded to make the short tale (*povest'*) the dominant genre of the period. Influenced by the general tradition of soul-felt confessional literature à la St. Preux or Werther and by the specific contact with the narrative devices of Madame de Genlis, Karamzin injects his own personality into these tales, expounding his own ideas on literature and life.

In the article "What Does the Writer Need?" Karamzin provides an aesthetic rationalization for this interpolation of his personal, subjective world into the fictional world of his characters. While the tone of this short article is delicate and appropriately tender, it belies its intent. These are words "mixed with blood—that can kill," to adapt Pasternak's line. Karamzin begins by admitting that a writer needs talent, knowledge, and intellect but, more than these natural endowments, he "must possess . . . a good, tender heart" if his work is to last. The "heart" is Karamzin's word for sensibility, which is the core of creativity for the sentimental artist; every aesthetic concept radiates from it as spokes from a wheel. Art originates in the individual writer's emotional perceptivity or emotional impression, and the elaboration of the art proceeds through often illogical juxtapositions, random associations, and mystical correspondences to create a statement on life. Consequently, "The creator is always depicted in his creations and frequently—against his will." This seems illogical, Karamzin admits, but only because the act of creation is irrational, arising from inspiration, enthusiasm, and imagination to appear as a peculiarly unique vision of the artist's inner world and experiences. The writer who seeks to create for all eternity must ask himself *"What sort of a person am I?"* because he is limning his "soul and heart" in his works. He is the subject of each work, a microcosm and macrocosm at once; if successful, his particular perception will have—in Kant's term—a subjective universal validity.

The second theme of this article concerns the purpose of literature. It is not enough that the artist be a man of sensitivity and sympathy; he must be sensitive and sympathetic to the "good." Then, if his "soul can rise to a *passion for the good,* can nourish within itself a sacred *desire for the general welfare,*" he can "boldly invoke the Parnassian goddesses" with some hope of success.

There is a deep seriousness in this appeal for truthfulness on the artist's part. This "passion for the good" is a moral imperative which ennobles art and enables it to bring a moral blessing to man. In this regard, Dostoevsky relates the anecdote of the heavily mantled, venerable Parisian who walked the lonely streets of Paris in the depths of the night. When he would come upon a passerby, he would throw open his garment, revealing to the shocked bewilderment of the viewer a starkly nude body. Karamzin threw open the cloak and, for the most part, revealed a body finely clothed to conceal the defects of humanity. Sometimes, however, in spite of Karamzin and because of his truthfulness, the nude body of man's sensual nature is glimpsed.

"Mixed with blood"—but blood of the beast that had been slain or, at least, mortally wounded. The central concept of classicism, which had dominated Russian literature from the 1740's, was that of rationalism, perceiving and explaining the explainable. Each stage of the classical creative process, from the imitation of the ancients to the prescriptions of *bon sens,* is rationally plotted, functioning somewhat like a modern conveyor belt. Beginning with the plotting-board idea and running through a logical elaboration, everything is carefully and artfully prepared: the reasoned response, the controlled delirium, the appropriate style and language. Karamzin challenged this classical aesthetics in theory and practice. In place of rationalism, he emphasized sensibility, a sensuous approach to art that moved by means of emotions, impressions, subjective reactions toward an emotional and subjective expression. In place of the classical craftsman or artisan of the word, he placed the "creator," who sometimes mysteriously, sometimes illogically, sometimes intuitively, creates a world in his own image, a unique world of illusion and imagination which has all the force of reality. And, finally, the artist, sublimely contiguous to God, brings the sacred to the profane, exhorts man to live by *his* truths and to follow *his* divine voice.

Theory is a rationalization of art. Fortunately, in the nineties Karamzin exemplified various facets of this theory in a series of short tales which captured the fancy of the Russian reading public and had an undeniable influence on future developments in Russian literature. The most popular of these tales was "Poor Liza," and while it is hard for the cynical modern reader to believe, young Muscovites, men and women, wended their way to the pond near the Simonov Monastery and there inscribed their names on the old oaks surrounding it and shed tears over the tragic fate of the poor peasant girl.

Now, conscious of youthful naïveté, we only smile sympathetically at the seduction of innocence and in our maturity find
that Liza's innocence had masked ignorance and the seduction
had masked self-delusion.

"Poor Liza" is a tale of "the most powerful and at the same
time the most common passion in its varied activities," told by
an emotional and imaginative man who sees, beyond this
prosaic seduction, the weakness and perversity of man and the
hypocrisy and banality of his society. These judgments are
validated by the narrator, who acts as interpreter, interpolator,
and commentator, and largely in his own person introduces
the *belle âme,* the sentimental personality, to Russian literature. In all of the other tales, to a greater degree in "Natalie,
the Boyar's Daughter" and "The Island of Bornholm" and to a
lesser degree in "Julia," the narrator's experiences and personality dominate the tales which, he insists, are true, taken from
life, and serve as a valid commentary upon it.

Let us look at the sentimental personality as it appears in
"Poor Liza." Not until the very end of the tale are we told that
the narrator has heard the history of Liza from her lover,
Erast. Up to this point, we have been led to believe that the ac-
count of the seduction and its elaboration has come only from
the omniscient narrator. Why has the narrator withheld this
information? I would suggest that this information is deliberately withheld to obscure the line of demarcation between
Erast and the narrator and to emphasize the priority of the
narrator's observations and philosophy. Except for the factual
details of this tale, the narrator is primarily responsible for the
exposition and the philosophical remarks and conclusions.
Indeed, it must be so if literature is the portrait of the writer's
"heart and soul."

With this in mind, the lyrical introduction takes on new
dimensions: It introduces the narrator, describes a familiar
town and site, and juxtaposes in a highly selective and poetic

way those localities which will play a significant role in the tale. The narrator is a solitary individual who wanders the Moscow environs to find "new, pleasant sites or new beauties in the old." He is an impressionable man of a new type, one who responds not so much to an ideal landscape of nature, balanced, harmonious, and precisely defined, but to the Gothic towers of the Simonov Monastery, to the distant hills of Moscow, to the "terrible masses of homes and churches," to the majestic and awesome picture of nature. The vast, illimitable landscape, with its mixture of the sacred and profane, appeals to him and he captiously finds a discordant note in the "simple sad songs" of the idyllic young shepherds. He is an enigmatic man who in the "gloomy days of autumn" comes to the Simonov Monastery "to grieve together with nature." And to dream—of sad scenes and gloomy events, of the death that autumn suggests, of the "bitter tears" of the young monk, of the tragedies that Moscow has witnessed. He is a sensitive man, who loves "those objects, which touch [his] heart and force [him] to shed tears of tender sorrow."

Here, specifically and concisely, are some of the major characteristics of the sentimental personality: He is a solitary who has perhaps rejected the crass society of man for the solacing comfort of nature: he is impressionable, a man who responds to a new concept of nature, rude, wild, picturesque in the style of Salvador Rosa, whose scenes stress broken lines, vast and vague distances and deserted places; the idyllic landscape of happy peasants is distrusted and dismissed. He is imaginative, creating sad tales of imaginary incidents in a deserted monastery. And, most of all, he is a man of acute sensitivity, who reacts with his tears not to worldly cataclysms but to those obscure, unnoticed, forsaken individuals who have suffered innocently. "Tears," Karamzin tells us, "always flow from a love of goodness and nourish it." To improve manners not by laughter but by tears occasioned by pictures of traduced innocence is the narrator's moral imperative.

Another vital function of this introduction is to make the point that this is a true tale; the environs of Moscow were real and familiar to all of Karamzin's contemporary readers. The Moscow locale is quite precisely, if poetically, described: the Simonov Monastery on a hill overlooking the river, the great town mass itself, the heavy trade on the Moscow River, the oak groves, the Danilov Monastery and the Sparrow Hills in the blue distance. More than a simple attempt to provide local color, these references suggest some of the major themes and events of the unfolding tale. Here is the Rousseauistic distinction between the city, described in critical terms: "a terrible mass of homes and churches," "greedy Moscow" living on the fruitful produce of the Russian empire; and the countryside, described in idyllic terms, "fertile, verdant, flowering." A parallel distinction will be drawn in the conflict of the sophisticated, destructive hero and the innocent, naïve peasant girl. The narrator, like Erast, leaves the turmoil of Moscow to seek the solacing beauty of the countryside, only to find there the same histories of sorrow and suffering.

The Simonov Monastery is almost the geographic center of the tale's action and the first identifiable site for the reader. For the Muscovite reader this monastery, with its long walls, spired towers reaching to a height of 130 feet, and holy well which attracted the sick to its miracle-working waters, always had an air of mystery about it. Karamzin describes it as it appeared in the latter half of the century, when its properties had been partly secularized by a law of the sixties and partly evacuated during the plague of the seventies; it was deserted, its walks and ruined graveyards overgrown with grasses. In a larger sense Karamzin here touches upon another significant theme of the tale, the passing of the old, divinely ordained order and the coming of the new, secular way of life, in which man, not God, directs his own destiny and creates a humane world of human values. This passing world order is exemplified in the vignettes of the dying monks and in the sufferings of Moscow in the seventeenth century when she "awaited succor from God alone." God may still be alive at the end of "Poor Liza," but He is less severe and stern, more merciful and forgiving, than the God who formerly dwelt within these monastery walls.

The many small details of the lyrical introduction provide the reader with a hint of things to come. The Moscow River will bring Erast to Liza on that fateful morning, the oak grove will be their trysting place, and the "groan," to which the narrator gave heed and which caused his heart to shudder and tremble, is perhaps the groaning which the superstitious peasant at the end of the tale hears at night and identifies as Liza's call from the grave. These features, artfully drawn from the narrator's own personal vision, are the substance of art for Karamzin and, while he speaks specifically of the poet in the "Preface" to *Aonides,* his observations could very well be applied to the prose writer, for "these very features, these details and this, so to speak, personality assure us of the truth of the descriptions and often deceive us; but such deception is the triumph of art."

This tale relates in a very significant way to the larger literary and cultural movement. It is not the philosophical profundity or social scope that matters, although I believe both aspects of Karamzin's prose contributions have been undervalued, but the sense of total commitment of the author to a new type of art, a new sense of values, a new concept of society, which pervades his works. Karamzin represents one of the most important literary forces in the last years of the eighteenth century working to shift the dominant classical current, which flowed into Russia from France and Germany, in a direction which would more truly reflect the wide and varied experiences of the Russian writer in style and theme.

"Poor Liza" is not only an open attack upon classicism but, woven into the character of Erast, is a castigation of the obvious irreality of previous literature and a condemnation of its harmful effects. In the opening of the tale, Karamzin mentions the "sad history" of "unhappy Moscow" but refuses to elaborate upon it; he is "most of all" attracted by the history of poor Liza, an insignificant peasant girl. The choice is clear and quite in keeping with his admonition to the young poet in the "Preface" to describe "the first impressions of love, friendship, the delicate beauties of nature, rather than the destruction of the world, a general conflagration of nature, and so on in this fashion." Karamzin will not deal with the grandiose themes and grand characters of classical epic and tragedy, preferring the real histories of real, if ordinary, people. Thus, the fiction of a true incident told to the narrator by his friend, the use of local color, and the exact description of the site of Liza's cottage, "some seventy sazhens from the monastery walls," all suggest the tale's reality, its nearness to the reader, and the possibility of its happening to the reader. Karamzin occasionally even toys with a favorite device of the classical writer, the allusion to Greek and Roman deities. When Erast appears at Liza's cottage and takes the first steps in his banal seduction, he is offered milk, and Karamzin observes that "nectar from the hands of Hebe could not have seemed tastier to him." And, when Liza and Erast kiss in the oak grove, Karamzin humorously observes that the "chaste, bashful Cynthia did not hide from them behind a cloud." Both allusions seem to me facetious uses of an old classical device: one, the comparison of a simple peasant girl to a Greek goddess, and the other, the humorous interpolation of the goddess of fertility in a scene of "pure and innocent" amorous dalliance.

35

Introduction

The critique of classicism is more intricately involved in the characterization of Erast. The chronology of the tale helps us to understand a significant confrontation of Erast with his society. If we accept the time of writing of "Poor Liza" (*ca.* 1791) as contemporary with the narrator's peregrination through the Moscow countryside, we can place the time of events in the early sixties ("Some thirty years before the beautiful, dear Liza had lived in this cottage with an old woman, her mother."). It was a period of interest in the classical *romans d'aventure,* of the rising interest in classical pastoral poetry, of the height of classical influences in general. In his fictionalized autobiography, "A Knight of Our Time," Karamzin describes these novels as "a picture of love" where the "heroes and heroines, despite the many temptations of fate, remain virtuous." And he is quite right, for these are stories of high-born men and maids who are separated by fate from their loves and who suffer indescribably difficult adventures before they are reunited, as pristinely pure as on the day of their birth. Another popular genre at that time was the pastoral poem or idyll. A. P. Sumarokov, the classical dramatist and most popular Russian exponent of the idyll, depicted for the delight of his aristocratic audience the love of innocent shepherdesses and none too innocent shepherds in arcadian surroundings. A glorification of physical pleasure runs through these pastoral poems, and the shepherdess's sense of shame, rather than a Christian sense of sin, is the major deterrent to sexual license.

It is this tradition that the narrator has in mind when he says of Erast, "He often reads romances, idylls, had a rather lively imagination and frequently transported himself in fancy to those times (which may or may not have existed), where, if we are to believe the poetizers, all people blithely wandered through the meadows, bathed in pure springs, kissed each other like turtledoves, rested beneath roses and myrtles, and spent all their days in happy idleness." This literature dealt with unreal situations unrealistically and its influence was sometimes pernicious. Immersed in this literary tradition and corrupted somewhat by the crass sensuality of his aristocratic society, Erast weaves an idyllic love affair of his and Liza's emotions. Although he professes love for her "sensitive, innocent soul" and convinces himself that he can live with her as "a brother with his sister," he is actually acting out the role of a shepherd in love with his shepherdess. Erast deludes himself and destroys Liza because no return is possible to that arcadian dream; in the narrator's mind, there is little, if any, belief that it ever existed. Corrupted by a society that taught him the hypocritical methods of sensual love, Erast is corrupt and hypocritical. "Weak," he fears the censure of society; "frivolous," he decides to flee society to find that "which his heart had long sought." Unfortunately, Liza is a real person, capable of deep and powerful affection; she has not read these novels and idylls, nor has she been nurtured in that dishonest society. Liza is the victim of both influences.

However, it is not only in the mockery of certain classical devices and in pointing out the pernicious influences of a crass sensualism upon certain individuals that Karamzin carried out his attack. In a larger sense he opened the portals of the nineteenth century by popularizing a new type of individual, the sentimental *belle âme,* who developed in varied directions in subsequent literature: the alienated man of Pushkin's *Eugene Onegin,* the fatal hero of Lermontov's *A Hero of Our Time,* and the charmingly pristine and altruistic heroines of Pushkin and Turgenev. Karamzin built his characterization upon those already popular in France, Germany, and England: St. Preux, Werther, Pamela, and Clarissa, who had become increasingly familiar to the Russians in the latter part of the century. He clothed them in Russian dress, had them act in a Russian environment and react to Russian social pressures. This captured the fancy of the Russian readers, who were able to identify with his creations and to bridge, as Karamzin puts it in "On the Book Trade and Love of Reading in Russia," the "great distance between the author and reader" which separated the average Russian from Rousseau or Richardson.

The characters of classical literature, the Chimenes and Neros of French tragedy or their Russian counterparts, the Semiras and Dimitriis of Sumarokov, are "monolithic" creations, people of a singular, unique passion, carried to an extreme, until out of control it provokes its own downfall through the conflict with society, civil codes, or a religious order. Emotions for the classicist lead to passions which can be destructive to the individual and society and, consequently, must be controlled.

Karamzin perceived, however dimly, a new, sensual approach to man and depicted a broad gallery of varied prose portraits to illustrate it. Man is not a simple rational being but a complex creature subject to his emotions and impulses, living in a world "where good and evil, where truth and error carry on a bloody struggle." [12] Karamzin joins the battle, convinced that goodness and truth, rooted in the intuitive, emotional side of man, will win. Basically, this is a Rousseauistic view of man: emotions can guide the individual toward virtue if they are properly trained and exercised and if they are not corrupted by the evil and error of society. This emphasis on the intuitive, subjective ego rises quite naturally from Karamzin's aesthetic and philosophical beliefs and just as naturally gives rise to the main problems faced by Karamzin's characters. The acutely sensitive man, who strives for a good

12. N. M. Karamzin, "Filalet k Melodoru" ("Philaletus to Melodorus") *Izbrannye sochineniia* ("Selected Works") (Moscow-Leningrad: Izdatel'stvo Khudozhestvennaia literatura, 1964), II, 258.

which he intuitively comprehends, finds himself alienated from his society, whose standards are perhaps more urbane, more permissive, and—more hypocritical. Yet, the man of sensibility finds in his emotions a redemptive grace, for they unite him with others of similar perception, bring him into closer contact with nature, whose beauty reflects the virtue of its Creator, and unite him with God, the ultimate source of all goodness and virtue.

The stress upon the emotional nature of man and the correctness of emotional judgments opened a Pandora's box. The Cartesian world of the seventeenth century, where society, morality, and religion were precisely ordained and defined, gave way to a vague world where the individual, drawing upon his own experiences and formulating his own judgments, set his own course. He no longer sought to satisfy the customs and mores of the social, moral, or religious orders; standards of righteousness no longer were externalized; man had to decide for himself and then assume responsibility for his actions. To a greater or lesser degree, the affirmation of the right of the individual to choose for himself is a major element of the Karamzin gallery of portraits, and, inevitably, the individual finds himself adrift in a turbulent sea of varied and conflicting choices and, often, in conflict with society.

Liza is an honest, responsible child of nature who suddenly discovers the emotion of love. But she immediately accepts it as the most important element in her life, obeys its dictates, and welcomes its responsibilities. This passion changes her life: She deceives her mother by not revealing Erast's declaration of love; she arranges secret assignations with him; she refuses the peasant marriage her mother had arranged; she becomes a sexual plaything of her beloved. All in the name of her love for Erast. When Erast's treachery becomes clear, she commits suicide, fully conscious that her love for Erast has led her to abrogate her filial, moral, and social responsibilities.

Introduction

The fate of the young lovers in "The Island of Bornholm" is rooted in the same choice and is equally terrible: The young man is condemned to wander as an external exile and the young woman to squander her life as an eternal prisoner. While the events of the tale are murky, it seems possible that they are brother and sister (he has been forced to leave by a "parental oath," perhaps of the "gray-haired old man," and she tells the narrator that she will "die as his tender, unfortunate" perhaps daughter?) and that the "sacred law" which they have violated is that of incest. The song of the singer of Gravesend pleads for the primacy of "innate feelings," of a love that arises without heed to "laws." Whatever the "sacred law" may have been, the lovers have come into violent and disastrous conflict with society because they followed the natural dictates of their hearts.

Natalie, the boyar's daughter, is the only character who follows the dictates of passion and who does not end in tragedy or near-tragedy. And the explanation is obvious. In this tale Karamzin is indulging in a bit of "sentimental" irony —if I may be allowed to add another variation to the already overcrowded catalogue—detaching himself from the scene of action to comment ironically on one of the beloved clichés of the "cult of sensibility," love at first sight. From the initial moment when Natalie spies her lover in church and says "It is he!" until the happy conclusion, Karamzin pokes fun at the irrationality of intuitive love, which springs from the unprobed subconscious and is controlled by nature and God for predestined beneficent ends. He draws upon the supreme "ironicist" of the eighteenth century, Laurence Sterne, to parody other sentimental conventions. A favorite device of the Englishman is the contrast between the real and the ideal, the practical and the visionary, and, thus, the supposition of a prosaic reader who is invoked to confirm—at least hopefully —the whimsical Parson's visionary ideals. "Natalie, the Boyar's Daughter" utilizes this technique to such an extent that it becomes a colloquy between a cynical, pragmatic reader and an unselfish, sentimental narrator. Thus, the narrator seeks permission of the reader to describe the petty details of Natalie's life or, in the face of the reader's doubts, justifies Natalie's frequent visits to church with the explanation, "Where else, if not in a church, could a curious lass steal a glance at people?" Karamzin spoofs other sentimental ideals and devices: the love of animals (the grandmother even allows a butterfly to find refuge on her nose); the frequent tears ("and suddenly a diamond-like tear sparkled in her right eye—then also in her left—and both rolled forth—one dropped on her bosom, and the other hesitated on her blushing cheek"); the exact description of irrelevant details and the sentimental style of periphrasis ("The green carpets of spring and summer were covered with a powdery snow, the terrible tsaritsa of the cold ascended her icy throne . . . that is, winter came"); and so on. The reader can conclude, quite logically, that only in such a world—of irony, parody, and burlesque—can a naïve and simple heart find happiness with little suffering and no tragedy.

The real world will always contain snares and delusion, traps and concealments, for those who follow the dictates of their heart. The heroine of "Julia" finds this out, to her sorrow and suffering. Set in the contemporary society of Moscow, this amusing tale is one of Karamzin's finest creations. In describing the education of the *belle âme,* he avoids the excesses of the sentimentally tragic ending and the extremes of sentimental characterization, maintaining a balance between spoof and seriousness. At the end of the tale, Aris defines Julia's character: "You were born to be virtuous; the immodest desire to please, the fruit of an injudicious upbringing and bad examples, produced your momentary aberrations." She typifies the emotional individual, who always obeys the dictates of the heart and constantly seeks to fulfill its emotional demands. However, her natural goodness, an innate concept of good and evil, saves her. The pressures of the nearly tragic experience with Prince N* force Julia to mature, to balance her emotional drive with some rational wisdom, to cease being a mere slave of society, and to seek the real goals to which her feelings can lead. After her marriage to Aris and in the boring solitude of the country, she describes well the pitfalls of the emotional life: "Ah, the human heart is insatiable; it constantly desires something new, new impressions, which like the morning dew refresh its inner feelings and give them new strength." Julia diagnoses the malaise of the sentimentalist: He is constantly seeking new emotional outlets, he is constantly seeking emotional experiences for the sake of the experience and not for some eternal end. The old religious concept of life as sacrifice, but with a promise of ultimate resurrection, was dying out, and man, alone, had to reconstruct new values to sustain his life. Karamzin tries to indicate the new; it is "virtue," "goodness," or an active exemplification of these ideals in daily conduct. Emotions and feelings guided by some common sense must lead to this secular perspective and, however menial or isolated a life may be, if it is conducted so as to demonstrate the goodness of man, it must be good. However, it is the sentiments, not reason alone, which help lead to this view.

If the emotional man is virtuous and desires the good, why does this exercise of emotions often lead to tragedy? Here, as Karamzin pointed out in his essay, "Philaletus to Melodorus," corruptive and false principles come into play: The materialistic and hedonistic standards of society create "evil" and "error" to entrap and ensnare goodness and truth. This "evil" and this "error" are personified in Erast, Prince N*, and Count N.N., the author of "My Confession," and they trigger the tragic "bloody struggle." However, it must be remembered that Karamzin stresses the responsibility of each individual for his actions and attempts to illustrate the psychological process by which such an individual arrives at this decision. Thus, it is true that Liza is betrayed by Erast, but her naïve innocence and lack of experience with evil contribute to her fate; Julia, egotistical, vain, lacking moral perspicacity, has been deluded by Prince N*, but the fault is still placed on her shoulders. The *bêtes noires* of Karamzin's prose make the virtuous question their own motives and probe their own actions and, in this confrontation, the corrupt reveal the corruptibility of man.

The emotions of the corrupt have atrophied or been stunted by an intense egoism. Erast is not an evil man—he has a "good heart"—but he is weak and frivolous. In the denouement, his own material well-being takes precedence over his vows and promises to Liza, and he sacrifices her for wealth, social position, and the approbation of society. Prince N* is a frank hedonist, aristocratic, rich, handsome, and his heart is such as Julia described, "insatiable," constantly seeking new pleasures, new excitations, new emotional experiences. The prince loves "only for the pleasure of love" and not to find some sentimental eternal verity. As the romantic heroes of a later period, the greater the obstacle to that love, the more pleasure is found in the pursuit. Julia was worthy game as the reigning queen of Muscovite society but as the virtuous wife of a virtuous nobleman—that is, as the symbol of a moral code restricting Prince N*'s actions—the chase is far more difficult, far more challenging, and, if successful, far more rewarding to his own ego. The prince lives for himself alone and this intense egoism has vitiated the natural emotional drive toward goodness and virtue. The tragedy is that society not only creates such individuals but tolerates and even venerates them.

The bitter culmination of this corruptive influence is evident in the portrayal of Count N.N., in whom egoism blossoms into a callous cynicism and like some exotic anthropophagous plant devours all in its way. Count N.N. is not an unexpected development, however, but simply the reverse of the coin, one side of which bears the graven image of the *belle âme* and the other, the cynical soul. God cannot exist without the Devil, nor the virtuous without the wicked. Throughout the nineties, Karamzin had been grappling quite honestly, if none too profoundly, with the Rousseauistic dilemma of the naturally good man's struggle with evil; in so doing he had become progressively more involved with and more interested in the darker side of life. This shift of emphasis is not only a counterbalance to his early sentimental optimism—which had been severely shaken by the shocks of the nineties, the dispersal of the Masons, the Thermidorean reaction in France, the repression of Catherine's last years, and the capriciousness of Paul's regime—but something more startling and original: the affirmation of negation, of pessimism, of cynicism, all inherent in the cult of sensibility. The man of emotions is acutely sensitive, acutely aware of the vulgarities of life, which like inane commercials assault him on all sides. He can retreat from them or become impervious to them, "tune them out" as it were, and find refuge in some form of stoicism. Or, however wounded, he can stand and fight with the only weapon available to him, criticism—a violent criticism of a society which spawns the evil and begets the horrors of a "civilized" life. This is what Karamzin chose to do, and his humorous portrayal of Count N.N.'s adventures has a deep seriousness to it: to understand the social and moral conditions which give rise to the "immoral imperative" of society and, perhaps, through such understanding, to change them.

Count N.N. is the Russian Marquis de Sade, whose basic dictum, "my own pleasure," might very well come from the pages of *Justine.* He is everything that the sentimentalist is not, a sensualist, a hedonist, unfaithful, dishonest, sly, and he confronts the sentimentalist's ideals at every turn to refute them. He mocks education, which should "adorn" the mind and refine the manners; he insults woman, desecrates religious symbols, violates friendship, and finds great pleasure in all of this, a rogue who delights in his roguery: "All the world seemed to [him] the indiscriminate play of a Chinese screen, all rules—a bridle for weak minds, all duties—an intolerable restraint." Here is the monster that Erast could have become, that Julia's "insatiable" heart portended, that Prince N* promises—a creature made insensate by the excessive exercise of his sensations, one who finds the novelty of experience and the shock of its effect to be the only purpose of his life. This is the Pandora's box and the creature that emerged from it.

The "divine" Count devotes himself to the seduction of women because "amorousity," the engagement in a love affair, occupies an otherwise empty life and gives it a purpose. But the variations are finite; after the first few liaisons, indifference threatens. The Count, however, proves the flexibility of his imagination by escaping into marriage and, after bankruptcy and divorce disrupt his happy immorality, the stage is set for his most audacious scheme. He allows his wife to remarry and then moves into her husband's house. What follows is an abrasive satire on sentimentalism, in which Karamzin sounds for the first time in his tales a note of violent anger, directed, oddly enough, not at the Count but at the naïve, ignorant, "beautiful soul," Emilia. Thrown into constant contact with the Count, Emilia, a thoroughly emotional creature, sensitive, sympathetic, and melancholy, is touched by his languid mien, moved by his tender letters, and amenable to his feigned sentimental ways. As Karamzin points out in his essay, "The Emotional and the Cold," the extreme character cannot be happy: The emotional individual is constantly lacerated by his own sensitivity while the stoic never really becomes totally involved in life. Emilia lacks that firm moral principle, arising from the exercise of reason, which would allow her to subordinate her immediate emotional satisfaction to some mediate general good. For this reason the sensitive fall prey to the insensate. Emilia once more succumbs to the Count and flees with him, comforting "herself with the thought that she was following the stirrings of an unconquerable feeling and that her love for [him] was heroic." This desecration of marriage, the violation of friendship and hospitality, the playing with emotions, the death of Emilia provoke nothing in the cynical Count but a "terrible dream" in an otherwise sound sleep.

Karamzin offers little hope to the man of emotions in these essays. To live by one's emotions means to come into conflict with society because society fosters and even adulates principles which are foreign to the man of sensibility: where he is frank, society extols deviousness; where he seeks a platonic union of souls, society admires sensuality; where he is altruistic, society praises egoism. The sentimentalists confront these contradictions and are destroyed or almost destroyed by them; Count N.N., on the other hand, joyfully accepts the role society offers him, mocks the spiritual suffering of the sentimentalist, and finds in his immoral imperative an effective *raison d'être*. Mr. Mendel says of his young charge: "Nature and fate have so arranged to make you a model of amiability and happiness; you are handsome, intelligent, rich, and aristocratic; sufficient for a brilliant role in the world! Everything else is not worth your labor." Deliberately or not, the "role" for which he is trained is that of a roué, whose motto, *"sauve qui peut*—let everyone think of himself—and it is sufficient!" is a debasement of the classical ideal of "self-interest," the sole necessity in a rationally conceived world. Self-interest, selfishness, a blind egoism—whatever the term for this towering concentration on the "self"—is the corrosive and destructive element in the milieu of Erast, Prince N*, and Julia.

46

But the world is not rational and this corrosion has under-mined the entire moral code of society. Egoism, immorality, materialism, ostentation parade as virtues and are venerated by society's members. Count N.N. revels in his reputation as a seducer and his "actions were copied and repeated quite faith-fully." The description of the Count's life is quite detailed and the point seems to be that he has looked closely at the moral code, understood its veneration of immorality, and has seen that an outward brilliance and a high social status excuse flagrant breaches in that code. If the politeness of society masks the fact that woman is a sexual toy, if the reputation of a wit excuses obscene and improper remarks, if a rake's noto-riety justifies his treatment of Emilia and the prince, then Count N.N. will be polite, witty, and notorious, and society will accept him as its darling. He points up the irrationalities of society and utilizes them to achieve his own base pleasures.

While this philosophical attitude is not quite as extreme as De Sade's "God or nullity," it flows from the same rational *abductio ad absurdum.* If the Count does not achieve the grandeur of the divine Marquis, he is at least a petty demon who views man as an insignificant nullity, a soulless creature to be manipulated or controlled for the demon's own ends. There is no god to be sought, no transcendental vision to be experienced; there is simply a sense of power that comes from exercising control over others, whether it be as a Lovelace in his youth or as a panderer in old age, or as one who through-out his life pricks the balloon of false ideals that society floats for its own amusement.

Count N.N. is the first Russian sketch in the long line of romantic portraits of the man in revolt. His own rational faculty has revealed to him the banality and sterility of the values that society venerates, and he strikes out to destroy them or to take advantage of them for his own use. Count N.N. is more than a stoic, for despite his slogan, "So be it," he questions or accepts only to pervert for his own satisfaction. As time goes on, this prototype of the romantic hero will become embittered, sullen, and far more dangerous; for he will feel himself thwarted and frustrated not only by society but by God, and his actions will then assume titanic proportions, to overthrow the universe and re-create it in his own image. Karamzin still wants to accept this world and its flawed society, but he has set the stage for the coming struggle and the coming greatness by grasping the essential dichotomies and ineffaceable contradictions within each individual. While he has given "things unknown . . . a local habitation and a name," the center of his vision is always man and his society.

Nineteenth-century literary specialists have treated Karamzin harshly, rather like the gentleman who seeks to demean, since he cannot dismiss, his humble parents. Their view of Karamzin as an unoriginal and unabashed purveyor of sentimental wares bought wholesale at the European market has given way in our century to a fairer evaluation. Boris Eikhenbaum, that fine critic whose humane insights are not obscured by his Formalist logic, justly remarked in an essay of 1916 that "we still have not read Karamzin carefully enough because we have not read him correctly. We have sought the letter but not the spirit." Karamzin did not simply garb the *schöne Seele* or *belle âme* in Russian ruffles and flounces; he did much more. He asked those embarrassing questions about man and society that give literature significance and, in a more talented writer, greatness. How can individual rights be squared with the overwhelming pressures of society? Can a faith in life be substituted for the death of faith? Why is beauty, often so divine, so demonically destructive? What are the rational and emotional fallacies of life? He looked truthfully, if not too deeply, at these problems and was disturbed by what he saw. He did not believe completely in his own simple solution, "love," any more than Dostoevsky believed completely in "faith," or Tolstoy in "reason," but he did not have to, for the fact that he posed these questions is "itself the miracle," and they have caused echoes throughout the nineteenth century. It might be well to conclude with a statement of Prince Viazemskii, Karamzin's godson and noted literary critic of the past century, who had, I think, something of this in mind when, some hundred years ago, he cautioned the Russians not to laugh at poor Liza, for "she is still related to us all."

Tales

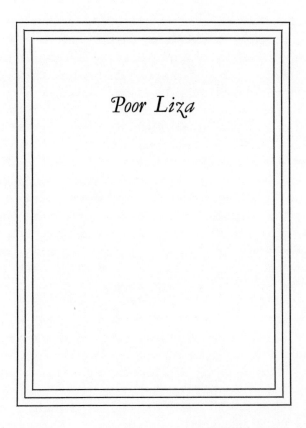

Poor Liza

PERHAPS NONE OF THE INHABITANTS of Moscow knows the environs of the town as well as I because no one frequents the fields more than I, no one wanders, without plan, without aim more than I—where the eyes lead—through the meadows and groves, over the hills and plains. Every summer I find new, pleasant sites or new beauties in the old.

But most pleasant of all for me is that place over which rise the gloomy, gothic towers of the Si—nov Monastery. Standing on this height, one sees on the right side almost all of Moscow, this terrible mass of homes and churches, which appears as a majestic amphitheater to the eyes: a magnificent picture, especially when the sun shines on it, when evening rays gleam from the countless golden cupolas, from the countless crosses rising toward the heavens! The fertile, dark-green, flowering meadows below, while beyond them, over yellow sands, flows the clear river, rippling beneath the light oars of fishermen's boats or murmuring beneath the rudders of the heavy barges, which ply their way from the most fruitful lands of the Russian empire and provide greedy Moscow with grain. On the other side of the river can be seen an oak grove, beside which innumerable flocks graze; there the young shepherds, seated in the shade of trees, sing simple sad songs and shorten in this way the summer days which are so monotonous for them. A little farther on, in the heavy verdure of ancient elms, the gold-domed Danilov Monastery glitters; still farther, almost on the edge of the horizon, the Sparrow Hills grow blue in the distance. On the left side can be seen vast, grain-covered fields, woodlets, three or four hamlets, and far away the village of Kolomensk with its tall palace.

I often come to this place and almost always meet spring there; I also come there even in the gloomy days of autumn to grieve together with nature. The winds wail fearfully among the walls of the deserted monastery, among the graves overgrown with tall grass, and through the dark corridors of the cells. Here, leaning on the ruins of the gravestones, I hearken to the dull groan of time, engulfed by the abyss of the past—a groan which causes my heart to shudder and tremble. Sometimes I enter the cells and in my imagination depict those who had lived here—sad pictures! Here I see a gray-haired elder, kneeling before the crucifixion and praying for a quick dissolution of his earthly fetters because all his life's pleasures have disappeared, all his feelings, except those of illness and weakness, have died. There a young monk—with a pale face, with a

54

languid glance—looks at the field through the grating of the window, sees the cheerful little birds, freely sailing in the airy sea, looks—and bitter tears flow from his eyes. He languishes, withers, wastes away—and the doleful peal of the bell announces his untimely death. Sometimes I examine on the gates of the temple the depiction of the miracles which took place in this monastery; here fish fall from the heavens to sate the inhabitants of the monastery, besieged by innumerable foes; here the image of the Mother of God turns the enemy to flight. All this brings once more to mind the history of our fatherland—the sad history of those times when the ferocious Tatars and Lithuanians devastated with fire and sword the environs of the Russian capital and when unhappy Moscow, as a defenseless widow in her cruel calamities, awaited succor from God alone.

But most of all the recollection of the mournful fate of Liza, poor Liza—attracts me to the walls of the Si—nov Monastery. Ah! I love those objects which touch my heart and force me to shed tears of tender sorrow!

Some seventy sazhens from the monastery walls, beside a little birch grove, amid a green meadow, stands an empty cottage, without doors, without window frames, without a floor; the roof rotted and collapsed long ago. Some thirty years before, the beautiful, dear Liza had lived in this cottage with an old woman, her mother.

Liza's father was a rather well-to-do villager because he loved work, tilled the soil well, and always led a sober life. But soon after his death, his wife and daughter became poor. The lazy hands of the hired help cultivated the fields badly and the grain did not yield good harvests. They were forced to lease their land and at a very cheap price. In addition, the poor widow, almost constantly shedding tears over the death of her husband—because peasant women also know how to love!— day by day grew weaker and was quite unable to work. Only

Liza—who was fifteen years old on her father's death—only Liza, without sparing her tender youth, without sparing her uncommon beauty, labored day and night—she spun flax, knitted stockings, picked flowers in the spring and gathered berries in the summer—and sold them in Moscow. The sensitive, good old woman, seeing the indefatigability of her daughter, often clasped her to her weakly beating heart, called her God's gift, her benefactress, the comfort of her old age, and she prayed to God that He would reward her for all that she was doing for her mother. "God gave me hands to work," said Liza. "You fed me at your breast and cared for me when I was an infant; now my turn has come to care for you. Only cease your grieving, cease your weeping; our tears will not bring Father back." But frequently tender Liza could not restrain her very own tears—ah! She remembered that she had had a father and that he was no longer living, but to calm her mother she tried to hide the sadness in her heart and to appear calm and cheerful.—"In that world, dear Liza," the grief-laden old woman answered, "in that world I shall cease crying. There, they say, everyone will be cheerful; I, of course, shall be cheerful when I see your father. Only I do not want to die now—what will happen to you without me? Who will take care of you? No, may God allow me first to find a place for you! Perhaps, a good man will soon be found. Then, my blessings upon you, dear children, I will cross myself and serenely lie down in the damp earth."

Two years had passed since the death of Liza's father. The meadows were covered with flowers, and Liza came to Moscow with lilies-of-the-valley. A young, well-dressed man of pleasant appearance encountered her on the street. She showed him her flowers—and blushed. "Are you selling them, lass?" he asked with a smile. "I am," she answered. "And how much do you want?" "Five kopecks." "That is much too cheap. Here is a ruble for you." Liza was astonished, ventured to glance at the young man—blushed still more and, lowering her eyes, told him that she would not take a ruble. "And why not?" "I don't want anything extra."—"I think that beautiful lilies-of-the-valley, plucked by the hands of a beautiful lass, are worth a ruble. If you will not take it, then here are five kopecks for you. I would like always to buy your flowers; I would like you to pick them only for me."—Liza gave him the flowers, took the five kopecks, bowed, and wanted to leave, but the stranger grasped her arm.—"Where are you going now, lass?" "Home." "And where is your home?"—Liza told him where she lived, told him and left. The young man did not want to restrain her, perhaps because some passers-by had hesitated and, looking at them, smiled slyly.

Liza, returning home, told her mother what had happened to her. "You did well in not taking the ruble. Perhaps this was some kind of wicked man. . . ." "Ah, no, Mother dear! I don't think so. He has such a good face, such a voice. . . ."—"Nevertheless, Liza, it is better to live by your own labors and to take nothing as a gift. You still do not know, my friend, the way evil people can harm a poor lass! My heart is always in my throat when you go to town; I always place a candle before the icon and pray to our Lord God that He might preserve you from all harm and misfortune." Tears welled up in Liza's eyes; she kissed her mother.

The next day Liza cut the very finest lilies-of-the-valley and again went to town with them. Her eyes quietly sought for something. Many wanted to buy flowers from her, but she answered that they were not for sale and looked now here now there. Evening came, she had to return home, and the flowers were thrown into the Moscow River. "Let no one possess you!" said Liza, with a feeling of sadness in her heart. Toward evening of the next day, she sat by the window, spinning, and in a low voice singing plaintive songs, when suddenly she jumped up and cried out: "Ah!" The young stranger stood by the window.

"What has happened to you?" asked her frightened mother, who sat beside her. "Nothing, Mother dear," Liza answered timidly, "I have just seen him."—"Who?" "That gentleman who bought the flowers from me." The old lady looked out the window. The young man greeted her so courteously, with such a pleasant manner, that she could think nothing but good of him. "Hello, good old woman!" he said. "I am very tired; don't you have some fresh milk?" Dutiful Liza, without waiting for her mother's reply—perhaps because she knew it beforehand—ran to the cellar, brought back a clean pail, covered with a clean, wooden lid—grabbed a glass, washed it, dried it with a white towel, poured and served it through the window, while she, herself, looked at the ground. The stranger drank it—and nectar from the hands of Hebe could not have seemed tastier to him. Anyone can guess that after this he thanked Liza and thanked her not so much with words as with his glances. Meanwhile the good-natured old woman had managed to tell him of her grief and her consolation—of the death of her husband and the sweet qualities of her daughter, of her industriousness and tenderness, and so on and so on. He listened to her attentively but his eyes were—is it necessary to say where? And Liza, timid Liza, looked at the young man every now and then; but lightning does not flash and disappear in the clouds as quickly as her pale blue eyes turned down in meeting his glance. "I would like," said he to the mother, "your daughter to sell her work to no one but me. In this way, there will be no need for her to go to town often, and you will not be forced to part with her. I myself can drop in on you from time to time." Here joy flashed in Liza's eyes, which she tried vainly to conceal; her cheeks glowed like a sunset on a clear summer evening; she looked at her left sleeve and picked at it with her right hand. The old woman willingly accepted this offer, not suspecting any bad purpose in it, and assured the stranger that the linen, woven by Liza, and the stockings, knitted by Liza, were incomparably fine and wore longer than any others.—It was getting dark, and the young man wanted to leave. "And how should we address you, good, compassionate master?" asked the old lady. "My name is Erast," he answered.—"Erast," said Liza quietly, "Erast!" She repeated this name some five times, as if trying to fix it in her memory. —Erast bade them farewell until the next meeting and left. Liza followed him with her eyes, while her mother sat pensive and, having taken her daughter's hand, said to her: "Ah, Liza! How fine and good he is! If your bridegroom would be such as he!" Liza's heart began to palpitate. "Mother dear! Mother dear! How could that be? He is a master, and between peasants. . . ."—Liza did not finish her sentence.

Now the reader should be informed that this young man, this Erast, was a rather wealthy nobleman, with a fair mind and a good heart, good by nature but weak and frivolous. He led a dissipated life, thought only of his own pleasure, sought it in worldly amusements but frequently did not find it: he grew bored and complained of his fate. The beauty of Liza had made an impression on his heart at the first meeting. He often read romances, idylls, had a rather lively imagination and frequently transported himself in fancy to those times (which may or may not have existed), where, if we are to believe the poetizers, all people blithely wandered through the meadows, bathed in pure springs, kissed each other like turtle doves, rested beneath roses and myrtles, and spent all their days in happy idleness. It seemed to him that he had found in Liza what his heart had long sought. "Nature summons me to its embrace, to its pure joys," he thought and came to the decision to leave society—at least for a while.

Let us return to Liza. Night came—the mother blessed her

daughter and wished her pleasant dreams, but this time her wish was not fulfilled: Liza slept quite badly. The new guest of her soul, Erast's image, appeared so lifelike before her that she awoke almost constantly, awoke and sighed. Sometime before the rise of the sun, Liza got up, went down to the bank of the Moscow River, sat on the grass, and, sunk in grief, looked at the white mists which rippled through the air and, rising upward, left glittering drops on the green cover of nature. Quiet reigned everywhere. But soon the ascending orb of day aroused all creation: the groves, the little bushes revived, the little birds took wing and began to sing, the flowers raised their heads to gorge on the vivifying rays of light. But Liza still continued to sit, sunk in grief. Ah, Liza, Liza! What has happened to you? Until now, awaking together with the little birds, together with them you reveled in the morning and a pure, joyful soul shone in your eyes, as the sun shines in the drops of heavenly dew; but now you are pensive and the general joy of nature is alien to your heart.—Meanwhile a young shepherd, playing a reed pipe, drove his flock along the bank of the river. Liza fixed her glance on him and thought: "If he, who now occupies my thoughts, had been born a simple peasant, a shepherd—and if he now drove his flock past me: ah! I would greet him with a smile and would say kindly: 'Hello, dear little shepherd! Where are you driving your flock? Here the green grass grows as well for your sheep, here the flowers grow red as well, you can wreathe a garland of them for your hat.' He would glance at me with a tender air—would take, perhaps, my hand . . . a daydream!" The shepherd, playing a reed pipe, passed by and with his varicolored flock disappeared behind the nearby hill.

Suddenly Liza heard the noise of oars—glanced at the river and saw a boat, and in the boat—Erast.

All her veins began to throb and, of course, not from fear. She got up, wanted to go, but was not able to. Erast jumped

60

onto the bank, walked up to Liza and—her daydream was in part fulfilled: because he *looked at her with a tender air, took her by the hand.* . . . And Liza, Liza stood with downcast glance, with fiery cheeks, with trembling heart—she was not able to remove her hand—she was not able to turn aside when he drew near to her wth his rosy lips. . . . Ah! He kissed her, he kissed her with such fervor that the entire universe seemed to be a flaming cauldron!

"Sweet Liza!" said Erast.—"Sweet Liza! I love you!" and these words resounded in the depths of her soul as heavenly, rapturous music; she scarcely dared believe her ears and. . . . But I cast my brush away. I shall only say that at this moment of rapture Liza's timidity disappeared—Erast realized that he was loved, loved passionately by a fresh, pure, ingenuous heart.

They were seated on the grass with only a small space between them—they looked each other in the eye, spoke to each other: "Love me!" and two hours seemed but an instant to them. Finally, Liza recalled that her mother might be worried about her. It was necessary to part. "Ah, Erast!" she said, "will you love me always?" "Always, sweet Liza, always!" he answered. "And will you take an oath on that?" "I will, dear Liza, I will!"—"No! I need no oath. I believe you, Erast, I believe you. Could you possibly deceive poor Liza? Surely this could not be?"—"It could not, it could not, sweet Liza!"—"How happy I am, and how glad dear Mother will be when she finds out that you love me!"—"Ah no, Liza! There is no need to say anything to her." "But why!"—"Old people are frequently suspicious. She will imagine something bad." "That could not happen."—"However, I beg you not to say a word of this to her."—"Very well. I must obey you, even though I would not like to hide anything from her."—They said farewell, kissed for the last time, and promised to see each other every day toward evening either on the bank of the river or in the birch grove, or somewhere near Liza's cottage, only surely, without fail, to see each other. Liza left but her eyes turned a hundred times to Erast, who still continued to stand on the bank and followed her with his eyes.

Liza returned to the cottage in a different state from the one in which she had left. Her face and all her movements revealed a heartfelt joy. "He loves me!" she thought and was delighted by the idea. "Ah, Mother dear!" Liza said to her mother, who had just awakened. "Ah, Mother dear! What a beautiful morning! How cheerful everything is in the field! Never have the larks sung so well, never has the sun shone so brightly, never have the flowers smelled so pleasant!" The old woman, leaning on her staff, went out to the meadow to enjoy the morning which Liza described in such charming colors. In actuality, it seemed exceedingly pleasant to her; her dear daughter had through her own cheer made all of nature cheerful for her. "Ah, Liza!" she said. "How fine is the Lord God's world! Threescore years have I lived in this world, but still cannot get my fill of the Lord's works; I cannot get my fill of the clear heavens, like a high tent, and of the earth which every year is covered with new grass and new flowers. It must be that the heavenly Tsar loves man very much to adorn this world so well for him. Ah, Liza. Who would want to die if we did not sometimes experience grief? Apparently, that is the way it must be. Perhaps we would forget our souls if tears never fell from our eyes." But Liza thought: "Ah! I would sooner forget my soul than my sweet friend!"

After this, Erast and Liza, fearful lest they break their promise, saw each other every evening (after Liza's mother had gone to bed) either on the bank of the river or in the birch grove, but most frequently beneath the shade of the hundred-year-old oaks (some eighty sazhens from the cottage)—oaks shadowing a deep, clear pond which had been excavated in ancient times. There the silent moon, through green branches, frequently silvered Liza's light hair with its rays, the zephyrs played with it as did the hands of her sweet friend; frequently these rays illumined in tender Liza's eyes a glittering tear of love, which was always dried by Erast's kiss. They embraced—but the chaste, bashful Cynthia did not hide from them behind a cloud: pure and virtuous were their embraces. "When you," said Liza to Erast, "when you tell me: 'I love you, my friend!' when you clasp me to your heart and gaze at me with your loving eyes, ah! then I feel so fine, so fine that I forget myself, I forget everything, except—Erast. It is strange! Strange, my friend, that I, without knowing you, could live serenely and happily! I do not understand this now, I think now that life without you is not life but sadness and boredom. Without your eyes the bright moon is dark; without your voice the nightingale's singing is boring; without your breathing the light breeze is unpleasant for me." Erast was delighted with his shepherdess—so he called Liza—and, seeing how much she loved him, he seemed more lovable to himself. All the glittering amusements of society seemed nothing in comparison with these pleasures, which the *passionate friendship* of an innocent soul provided his heart. With abhorrence he contemplated the contemptible carnality in which his emotions had previously reveled. "I shall live with Liza, as a brother with his sister," he thought, "I shall not misuse her love and I shall always be happy!" Injudicious young man! Do you know your own heart? Can you always answer for your actions? Is reason always the master of your emotions?

Liza insisted that Erast visit her mother frequently. "I love her," she would say, "and wish her well, and it seems to me that to see you is a great boon for anyone."—Actually, the old woman was always glad to see him. She loved to speak with him about her late husband and recount the days of her youth, how she met her sweet Ivan for the first time, how he came to love her, and the love, the harmony, in which she lived with him. "Ah! We never were able to see enough of each other—until that very hour when cruel death cut him down. He died in my arms!" Erast listened to her with unfeigned pleasure. He bought Liza's work from her and always wanted to pay ten times more than the designated price, but the old woman never took anything extra.

In this fashion several weeks passed. Once toward evening Erast had been awaiting his Liza for some time. Finally she arrived but so despondent that he was frightened; her eyes were red from weeping. "Liza, Liza! What has happened to you?" "Ah, Erast! I have been weeping!"—"Why? What is it?"—"I must tell you everything. A bridegroom has been proposed for me, the son of a wealthy peasant from a neighboring village; dear Mother wants me to marry him."—"And you agreed?"—"Cruel man! How can you ask? But I feel sorry for my dear mother; she has been weeping and saying that I do not want her serenity, that she will suffer torments at death if she cannot arrange a marriage for me while she is still alive. Ah! Dear Mother does not know that I have such a sweet friend!" Erast kissed Liza, said her happiness was the most important thing in the world to him, that after her mother's death he would take her to his own home and live inseparably with her in the village and in the dense woods as in paradise.—"However, you could not be my husband!" said Liza with a soft sigh.—"Why not?" "I am a peasant."—"You insult me. Most important of all for your friend is the soul, the sensitive, innocent soul—and Liza will always be closest to my heart."

She threw herself into his embrace—and at that moment her virtue was to be destroyed!—Erast felt an unusual stirring in his blood—Liza had never seemed so charming to him—her caresses had never moved him so strongly—her kisses had never been so ardent—she knew nothing, suspected nothing,

feared nothing—the darkness of evening nourished desires—
not one little star shone in the heavens—not a single ray could
illume the transgression. Erast felt a trembling within—Liza
also, not knowing why—not knowing what was happening to
her. . . . Ah, Liza, Liza! Where is your guardian angel?
Where—is your innocence?

In a minute the transgression was over. Liza did not understand her feelings; she was astonished and asked about them.
Erast was silent—sought words and could not find them. "Ah,
I am afraid," said Liza, "I am afraid at what happened to us! It
seems as though I am dying, that my soul. . . . No, I cannot
say this! . . . You are silent, Erast? You sigh? . . . My God!
What is it?"—Meanwhile lightning flashed and thunder
crashed. Liza began to tremble all over. "Erast, Erast!" she
said. "I am terrified! I am afraid that the thunder will strike
me down as a criminal!" The storm rumbled threateningly,
the rain poured from the black clouds—it seemed that nature
mourned the loss of Liza's innocence.—Erast tried to calm
Liza and led her back to the cottage. Tears rolled from her
eyes when she bade him farewell. "Ah, Erast! Assure me that
we will be happy as before!"—"We shall be, Liza, we shall
be!" he answered.—"May God grant it! I cannot but believe
your words: you know I love you! Only in my heart. . . . But
enough! Farewell! Tomorrow, tomorrow we shall see each
other again."

Their meetings continued: but how everything had
changed! Erast could not now be satisfied only with the innocent caresses of his Liza—only with her glances full of love—
only with the touch of her hand, only with a kiss, only with a
pure embrace. He desired more, more, and, finally, could
desire nothing—but he who knows his own heart, who has
reflected on the quality of his most tender pleasures, he, of
course, will agree with me that the fulfillment of *all* desires is
the most dangerous temptation of love. For Erast, Liza was no

longer that angel of virtue which previously had inflamed his imagination and ravished his soul. Platonic love gave way to feelings which he could not be *proud* of and which were no longer novel to him. In regard to Liza, she, having given herself to him completely, lived and breathed only for him; as a lamb she obeyed his will in all things and his pleasure was her happiness. She saw the change in him and often said to him: "Before you were gayer, before we were calmer and happier, and before I was not so afraid of losing your love!" —Sometimes, in parting with her, he said: "Tomorrow, Liza, I cannot meet you: important business has come up"—and every time she heard these words, Liza sighed.

Finally, she did not see him for five days in a row and she was greatly agitated; he arrived on the sixth day with a sad visage and said to her: "Dear Liza! I have to part with you for some time. You know that we are at war, I am in the service, my regiment is going on a campaign." Liza grew pale and almost fainted.

Erast caressed her, said that he would always love his sweet Liza and hoped on his return nevermore to be parted from her. She was silent for a long time, then she began to weep bitterly, grabbed his hand, and, looking at him with all the tenderness of love, asked: "You cannot remain?"—"I could, but only with the greatest shame, with the greatest stain on my honor. Everyone will hold me in contempt; everyone will loathe me, as a coward, as an unworthy son of the fatherland."—"Ah, if that is so," said Liza, "then go, go where God commands! But you might be killed." "Death for the fatherland is not terrifying, dear Liza."—"I shall die, as soon as you cease to exist."— "But why think of that? I hope to remain alive. I hope to return to you, to my friend."—"May God grant it! May God grant it! I will pray for this every day, every hour. Ah, why can I not read and write! You could inform me of everything that happens to you and I would write to you—of my tears!"

—"No, take care of yourself, Liza, take care of yourself for your friend. I do not want you to weep over me."—"Cruel man! You want to deprive me even of this comfort! No! Parted from you, I might possibly cease weeping when my heart has completely run dry."—"Think of the pleasant moment when we shall see each other again."—"I shall, I shall think of that! Ah, if it would only come quickly! Dear, sweet Erast! Remember, remember your poor Liza, who loves you more than her very self!"

But I cannot describe everything which they said on this occasion. On the next day their last meeting was to occur.

Erast also wanted to bid farewell to Liza's mother, who could not restrain her tears on hearing that her *affable, comely master* must go to war. He forced her to accept some money from him, saying: "I do not want Liza, in my absence, to sell her work, which according to our agreement belongs to me." —The old woman strewed blessings upon him. "May the Lord grant," she said, "that you will return to us unharmed and that I shall see you once more in this life! Perhaps by that time my Liza will have found a suitable bridegroom. How I would thank God if you would come to our wedding! When Liza has children, bear it in mind, master, you must be their godfather! Ah! I would very much like to live to see this!"—Liza stood beside her mother and did not dare look at her. The reader can easily imagine what she felt at this moment.

But what did she feel when Erast, embracing her for the last time, for the last time pressing her to his heart, said: "Farewell, Liza! . . ." What a touching picture! The morning glow, like a crimson sea, suffused the eastern sky. Erast stood beneath the branches of the tall oak, holding in his embrace his pale, languishing, grief-laden friend, who, in bidding farewell to him, bade farewell to her soul. All nature was silent.

Liza sobbed—Erast wept—he left her—she fell—rose to

her knees, lifted her hands toward heaven and looked at Erast, who walked away—farther—farther—and, finally, disappeared—the sun began to shine and Liza, forsaken, poor, fell into a dead swoon.

Liza regained consciousness—and the world seemed doleful and sad to her. All the delights of nature had disappeared together with the one dear to her heart. "Ah!" she thought, "why have I remained in this wilderness? What is there to restrain me from flying after my sweet Erast? The war does not terrify me; it is terrible here where my friend is not. I want to live with him, to die with him or by my death save his precious life. Wait, wait, dear one! I shall fly to you!"—She wanted now to flee after Erast but the idea: "I have a mother!" stopped her. Liza sighed and, bowing her head, she walked slowly toward her cottage.—From that time on her days were days of yearning and grief, which she had to hide from her tenderhearted mother: all the more did her heart suffer! It was only eased when Liza, withdrawing to the depths of the woods, could freely shed tears and lament over the separation from her sweet one. Frequently, the sad turtle-dove joined its plaintive voice to her lamentations. But sometimes—it is true, quite rarely—a golden ray of hope, a ray of comfort illumined the gloom of her sorrow. "When he returns to me, how happy I will be! How everything will change!" Her glance brightened with the idea, the rosy glow of her cheeks revived, and Liza smiled, like a May morning after a stormy night.—About two months passed in this way.

One day Liza had to go to Moscow to buy some rosewater with which her mother treated her eyes. On one of the main streets she came upon a magnificent carriage, and in the carriage she saw—Erast. "Ah!" Liza suddenly cried and rushed toward it, but the carriage drove by and turned into a court-yard. Erast got out and was almost on the porch of an enormous home when he suddenly felt himself in Liza's embrace.

He grew pale—then, without answering her outcries, took her by the hand, led her into his study, locked the door, and said to her: "Liza! Circumstances have changed; I am engaged to marry; you must leave me in peace and for your own serenity forget me. I loved you and now I love you, that is, I wish you all that is good. Here is a hundred rubles—take them"—he put the money in her pocket—"allow me to kiss you for the last time—and go home."—Before Liza could gather her senses, he led her out of the study and said to his servant: "Conduct this girl from the house."

My heart bleeds at this moment. I forget the man in Erast —I am prepared to curse him—but my tongue does not move —I look at the heavens, and a tear rolls down my face. Ah! Why am I not writing a novel rather than a sad true tale?

Thus, had Erast deceived Liza, in telling her that he was going into the army?—No, he actually had been in the army but, instead of doing battle with the enemy, he played cards and lost almost all his property. Peace was soon concluded, and Erast returned to Moscow burdened with debts. Only one way was left him to correct his situation—to marry an elderly, rich widow who had long been in love with him. He decided to do this and moved into her home, dedicating a sincere sigh to his Liza. But can all this excuse him?

Liza found herself on the street and in a state that no pen could describe. "He, he drove me out? He loves another? I am lost!"—These were her ideas, her feelings! A dead faint interrupted them for a time. A good woman who was walking along the street stopped beside Liza, who was lying on the ground, and tried to bring her back to consciousness. The unhappy girl opened her eyes—got up with the aid of this good woman—thanked her and walked away, not knowing where. "It is impossible to live," Liza thought, "it is impossible! O, if the heavens would fall on me! If the earth would swallow this poor one! . . . No! the heavens won't fall; the earth won't quake! Woe is me!" She left the town and suddenly found herself on the bank of the deep pond, beneath the shade of the ancient oaks, which had been quiet witnesses of her raptures several weeks before. These recollections disturbed her soul; the most terrifying spiritual torments were expressed on her face. But after several moments she seemed absorbed by a certain thought—she looked about her, saw the daughter of her neighbor (a fifteen-year-old lass) walking along the road, called to her, took the ten imperials from her pocket, and, giving these to her, said: "Dear Aniuta, dear little friend! Take this money to my dear mother—it has not been stolen—tell her that Liza is guilty before her, that I have concealed my love for a cruel man, for E., from her. . . . But why should you know his name?—Tell her that he has betrayed me, implore her to forgive me—God will help her— kiss her hand as I now kiss yours. Tell her that poor Liza ordered you to kiss her—tell her that I . . ." Then she threw herself into the water. Aniuta cried out, began to weep, but could not save her; she ran into the village—people came and dragged Liza out, but she was already dead.

Thus, beautiful in soul and body, she ended her life. When we meet again *there* in that new life, I shall recognize you, tender Liza.

She was buried near the pond, beneath the gloomy oak, and a wooden cross was placed on her grave. Here I frequently sit, pensive, leaning against the repository of Liza's dust; the pond ripples before my eyes, the leaves rustle above me.

Liza's mother heard of the terrible death of her daughter and her blood grew cold from the horror—her eyes closed forever.—The cottage became empty. The wind wails within it and the superstitious villagers, hearing the wind at night, say: "There groan the dead; there groans poor Liza!"

Erast was unhappy for the rest of his life. When he found

out about Liza's fate, he could not be comforted and considered himself the murderer. I became acquainted with him a year before his death. He, himself, told me this history and led me to Liza's grave.—Now, perhaps, they have become reconciled.

1792

Natalie,

the Boyar's Daughter

WHO DOES NOT LOVE THOSE TIMES when Russians were
Russians, when they were attired in their own dress, walked in
their own way, lived according to their own customs, spoke in
their own language and from their hearts, that is, they spoke
as they thought? At least I love those times; I love to fly on
the swift wings of imagination to that distant obscurity, to
seek my whiskered forefathers beneath the canopy of long-
decayed elms, to chat with them about adventures of ancient
times, about the character of the glorious people of Russia,
and to kiss tenderly the little hands of my great-grandmothers,

73

who cannot look enough at their respectful great-grandson, cannot speak enough with me, cannot cease admiring my mind, because I, in discussing old and new fashions with them, always grant preference to their caps and fur jackets over the present-day bonnets *à la* . . . and all the Gallic-Albion attire, glittering on the Muscovite beauties of the end of the eighteenth century. In this way (understandable, of course, to every reader), Old Rus is better known to me than to many of my fellow citizens, and if dark fate will not cut off my life's thread for several years, then, finally, even I shall not have room in my head for all the anecdotes and tales told me by the inhabitants of the past hundreds of years. To ease somewhat the load on my memory, I intend to inform my dear readers of a true tale or history, which I heard in the region of the shades, in the kingdom of imagination, from the grandmother of my grandfather, who in her time was considered quite eloquent and almost every evening told fairy tales to the Tsaritsa N.N. Only I am terrified to distort her tale; I am afraid that the old woman will rush on a cloud from that world and will punish me with her staff for my inferior eloquence. . . . Ah no! Forgive my rashness, magnanimous shade—you are incapable of such an action! In your earthly life you were meek and gentle, as a young lamb; your hand destroyed neither the mosquito nor the little fly and the butterfly always rested peacefully on your nose: consequently, is it possible that now, when you swim in a sea of indescribable bliss and breathe the purest ether of the heavens—is it possible that your hand would be raised against your obedient great-great-grandson? No! You will allow him unhindered to practice the praiseworthy trade of scribbling on paper, to create fables of the living and the dead, to try the patience of his readers and finally, like the constantly yawning god, Morpheus, to throw them on the soft sofas and let them sink into a

deep dream. . . . Ah! At this very moment I see an unusual
light in my dark corridor, I see fiery circles, which revolve
glittering and crackling and finally—Oh, miracle!—they reveal your image, an image of indescribable beauty, of indescribable majesty! Your eyes shine as suns; your lips are as
crimson as the morning glow, as the summits of snowy moun-
tains at the rise of the orb of day—you smile, as the young
creation smiled on the first day of being, and in rapture I hear
your *sweetly thundering* words: "Continue, my dear great-
great-grandson!" So, I shall continue, I shall; and, arming
myself with a pen, I shall sketch bravely the history of *Natalie, the Boyar's daughter.*—But first I ought to rest; the
rapture, which the appearance of my great-great-grandmother
induced in me, has wearied my spiritual strength. I put my pen
down for a few minutes—and let these inscribed lines serve as
an introduction and as a foreword!

In the capital city of the glorious Russian kingdom, in
white-stoned Moscow, lived Boyar Matvei Andreev, rich, intelligent, a loyal servant of the Tsar and, according to the customs of the Russians, a man of great hospitality. He possessed
many estates and was not a persecutor but a protector and defender of his poor neighbors—which in our enlightened times,
perhaps, few will believe, but which in the old times was not
considered a rarity. The Tsar called him his right eye, and the
right eye never deceived the Tsar. When he had to resolve a
serious litigation, he summoned the Boyar Matvei to help him,
and Boyar Matvei, putting a pure hand on a pure heart, said:
"This one is innocent (not according to such-and-such decree,
promulgated in such-and-such a year, but) according to my
conscience; this one is guilty according to my conscience"—
and his conscience always conformed to the truth and the
conscience of the Tsar. The affair was decided without delay:
the innocent one lifted a tearful eye of gratitude to heaven,

pointing at his good sovereign and the good boyar, while the guilty one fled into the deep woods to hide his shame from man.

Still, we cannot pass in silence one praiseworthy practice of the Boyar Matvei, a practice which is deserving of imitation in any century and in any kingdom: to wit, at each of the twelve major church holidays long tables, covered with clean table-cloths, were set up in his chambers, and the Boyar, seated on a bench beside his tall gates, invited all the passing poor to dine,† as many as could be seated in the Boyar's dwelling; then, having gathered the appropriate number, he returned to his house, and, assigning a seat to each guest, he himself sat down among them. In a moment, there appeared on the tables cups and dishes, and the aromatic steam of the hot food, like a white, delicate cloud, curled over the heads of the diners. Meanwhile the host chatted affably with his guests, learned their needs, gave them good counsel, offered his services, and, finally, made merry with them as with his friends. Thus, in ancient, patriarchal times, when human life was not so short, the old man whose head was adorned with honorable gray hairs enjoyed fully his earthly goods with his innumerable family—he looked about and, seeing in every face, in every glance, a lively expression of love and joy, was spiritually delighted.—After the dinner all the needy brethren, having filled their glasses with wine, exclaimed in unison: "Good, good Boyar and our father! We drink to your health! May you live contentedly for as many years as there are drops in our glasses!" They drank, and their grateful tears fell on the white tablecloth.

Such was Boyar Matvei, a loyal servant of the Tsar, a loyal friend of humanity. His sixtieth year had already passed, the

† Many old men assure me of the truth of this. [All notes indicated by symbols are those of Karamzin; all numbered notes are those of the translator.]

blood already ran slower in his veins, the quiet beat of his heart already proclaimed the coming of the evening of his life and the approach of night, but was the good man afraid of this heavy, impenetrable darkness in which man's days are lost? Was he terrified by the shadowy road, when his heart was good, when his deeds were good? He goes forward dauntlessly, he enjoys the last rays of the setting orb, he turns a satisfied glance at the past and with a joyful—an uncertain but nonetheless a joyful—presentiment steps out into the unknown.—The people's love, the Tsar's kindness were the reward of the old Boyar's virtues; but the crown of his happiness and joys was his dear Natalie, his only daughter. He long ago wept over her mother, who dropped off into her eternal sleep in his embrace, but the cypresses of conjugal love were strewn with the flowers of parental love—he saw a new image of the deceased in young Natalie, and, instead of the bitter tears of sadness, sweet tears of tenderness began to shine in his eyes. There are many flowers in the field, in the groves, and on the meadows green, but none comparable to a rose; the rose is the most beautiful of all; there were many beauties in white-stoned Moscow, for the Russian kingdom from time immemorial was considered the dwelling of beauty and pleasures, but no beauty could be compared to Natalie—Natalie was the most charming of all. Let the reader imagine the whiteness of Italian marble and the snows of the Caucasus: He still could not imagine the whiteness of her face—and fancying the color of Zephyr's mistress, he still could not fully conceive the crimson of Natalie's cheeks. I hesitate to continue the comparison in order not to bore the reader by repeating the obvious because in our affluent times the store of poetic similes for beauty has been quite exhausted and many writers chew their pens in vexation, seeking but not finding new ones. It is appropriate, however, to realize that the most devout elders, seeing the Boyar's daughter at mass, forgot their low bows while praying, and the most biased mothers granted her preference over their own daughters. Socrates said that physical beauty was always an expression of spiritual beauty. We ought to believe Socrates because he was, in the first place, a skillful sculptor (consequently, he knew the characteristics of physical beauty) and, in the second place, he was a wise man and a lover of wisdom (consequently, he knew spiritual beauty well). At least our charming Natalie had a charming soul, she was as tender as a turtledove, innocent as a lamb, sweet as the month of May; in short, she had all the qualities of a well-educated maiden although the Russians had not read Locke's *Concerning Education* or Rousseau's *Émile*—in the first place, for the reason that these still had not been born and, in the second place, because they hardly knew how to read and write—they did not read and educated their children as nature educates the little grasses and little flowers; that is, they provided food and drink, leaving all else to the whim of fate, but this fate was kind to them, and for the trust which they placed in her omnipotence she rewarded them almost always with good children, the consolation and support of their old days.

One great psychologist, whose name I do not really remember, has said that the description of the daily activities of man is the truest representation of his heart. At least I think so, and with the permission of my dear readers I shall describe how Natalie, the Boyar's daughter, passed her time from the rising to the setting of the beautiful sun. No sooner had the first rays of this majestic orb appeared from behind the morning cloud, pouring onto the still earth its liquidy, insubstantial gold, than our beauty awoke, opened her dark eyes, and crossing herself with her white satiny hand, bared to the tender elbow, arose, put on a delicate silk dress, a figured jacket, and, her dark-brown hair loosened, she walked up to the circular window of her high living quarters to look at the beautiful picture of a revivified nature—to look at gold-domed Moscow, from which the radiant day removes the misty cover of night and which, like some sort of enormous bird, awakened by the voice of morn, shakes off the glistening dew in the breeze—to look at the Moscow environs, on the gloomy, heavy, vast Marina Grove, which, like bluish, curling smoke, was lost to the gaze in the immense distance where all the wild beasts of the north then lived, where their terrible roar drowned out the melodies of the singing birds. On the other side the sparkling sinuosities of the Moscow River met Natalie's gaze, the flowering fields and smoking hamlets from which the diligent villagers with gay songs went to their chores—villagers who even to this day have not changed in the slightest; they dress in the same way, live and work as they formerly lived and worked, and amid all the alterations and guises, they still represent for us the real Russian physiognomy. Natalie watched, leaning against the window, and felt a quiet joy in her heart; she did not know how to praise nature eloquently, but she knew how to delight in it. She was silent and thought: "How fine is our white-stoned Moscow! How fine are her surroundings!" But Natalie did not think that she, herself, in her morning attire was most beautiful of all. Her young blood, excited by nocturnal fantasies, colored her tender cheeks with a crimson glow, the sun's rays played on her white face and, penetrating the dark, downy eyelashes, shone in her eyes more brightly than gold. Her hair, like dark, coffee-colored velvet, lay on her shoulders and on her white partially revealed bosom, but quickly a charming modesty, shamed before the sun itself, the breeze itself, the dumb walls themselves, covered it with a delicate cloth. Then she awakened her nurse, a devoted maidservant of her late mother. "Arise, Nanny!" said Natalie. "They will soon ring for mass." Nanny arose, dressed, called her young lady a wee early bird, washed her with spring water, combed her long hair with a white bone comb, braided it, and adorned the head of our charmer with a pearl fillet. Having thus put on their attire, they waited for the ringing of the church bells and, locking their room (so that no bad man would steal in during their absence), set off for mass. "Every day?" the reader will ask. Of course—such was the custom in the old days—only the cruel snowstorm in the winter or the pelting rain and thunder in the summer could restrain the beautiful maid from fulfilling this pious duty. Always standing in the corner of the refectory, Natalie zealously prayed to God and meanwhile looked stealthily to the right and left. In the old days there were neither clubs nor masquerades, where today one goes to see and to be seen; thus, where else if not in a church could a curious lass steal a glance at people? After mass Natalie always distributed several kopecks to the poor and went up to her parent to kiss his hand with tender love. The old man wept for joy, seeing that his daughter became better and sweeter day by day and he did not know how to thank God for such a precious gift, for such a treasure. Natalie sat down beside him either to embroider on a tambour or to weave lace, or to twist silk or to string a necklace. Her tender parent wanted to look at her work but instead looked at her and reveled in a silent tender feeling. Reader! From your own experience do you know parental feelings? If not, then recall at least how your eyes admired the gaily colored little carnation or the whitish jasmine which you had planted, with what pleasure you examined their colors and shadings and how you were gladdened by the thought: "This is my flower; I have planted it and nurtured it!" Recall and realize that a father looks at his sweet daughter even more happily and more happily thinks: "She is mine!"—After the heavy Russian dinner Boyar Matvei lay down to rest but allowed his daughter and her nanny to take a walk either in the gardens or in the large green meadow where today the *Red Gates* with their trumpeting Glory rise. Natalie plucked the flowers, admired the flying butterflies, was nourished by the fragrance of the grass, returned home happy and peaceful, and took up again her handiwork. Evening came—a new walk, new pleasure; sometimes her young girl friends came to share the cool of the evening with her and to chat about all sorts of trifles. The good Boyar, Matvei himself, usually talked with them if state or necessary domestic concerns did not occupy his time. His gray beard did not frighten the young beauties; he knew how to amuse them pleasantly and related the adventures of the God-fearing Prince Vladimir and his powerful Russian knights.

In the winter, when it was impossible to walk either in the garden or in the field, Natalie sleighed through the town and went to evening parties, where only the maidens were present, to amuse herself and make merry and in this innocent fashion to pass her time quickly. There the nannies and nurses concocted various amusements for their young ladies: they played blindman's buff, hide-and-seek, hid gold,[1] sang songs, were frisky without losing their decorum, and laughed without derision so that a modest and chaste dryad could always have been present at these evening parties. The late midnight hour parted the maidens, and charming Natalie in the embrace of darkness enjoyed a peaceful sleep, which youthful innocence always enjoys.

Thus lived the Boyar's daughter, and the seventeenth spring of her life had come; the little grasses had turned green, the flowers had bloomed in the field, the larks had begun to sing—and Natalie, seated in the morning in her room beneath the window, looked out at the garden, where the little birds fluttered from little bush to little bush and, tenderly kissing each other with their small beaks, hid in the depths of the

1. A type of game, accompanied by the song "I am hiding the gold."

leaves. The beauty noticed for the first time that they flew in pairs—they sat in pairs and concealed themselves in pairs. Her heart seemed to skip a beat as if some sort of sorcerer had touched it with his magic wand! She sighed—sighed a second and then a third time—she looked about her—she saw that no one was with her, no one except the old nurse (who dozed in the corner of the chamber in the beautiful spring sunshine)— she sighed again and suddenly a diamond-like tear sparkled in her right eye—then also in her left—and both rolled forth— one dropped on her bosom, and the other hesitated on her rosy cheek, on the small tender dimple which among sweet maidens is usually a sign that Cupid kissed them at birth. Natalie was sunk in grief—she experienced a certain sadness, a certain languor in her soul; everything seemed wrong to her, everything seemed out of joint; she got up and sat down again; finally she awakened her nanny, and told her that her heart was full of longing. The old woman began to make the sign of the cross over her sweet young lady and with certain *pious utterances* † to curse the man who had gazed at the beautiful Natalie with impure eyes or had praised her charms with impure tongue, not from a pure heart, not at the right time, because the old woman was convinced that she had been bewitched and that her inner longing came from nothing else. Ah, good old woman! Although you had lived long in the world, there was still much you did not know; you did not know what things happen and how they begin at a certain age among the daughters of our boyars, you did not know. . . . But, perhaps, the readers also (if at this time they still hold this book in their hands and have not fallen asleep)—perhaps the readers also do not know what misfortune suddenly overtook our heroine, what she sought with her eyes in her cham-

---

† For example, "Lord forgive me" and others similar to this, such as one can still hear even from our dear present-day nurses.

ber, why she sighed, wept, was sad. It is obvious that up until this time she was merry, like a free little bird, that her life flowed like a pellucid brook rushing over whitish pebbles between grassy, flowering little banks; just what was happening to her? Modest Muse, tell us!—From the heavenly azure vault and perhaps, from somewhere even higher, there descended a small, wee bird, a hummingbird, which fluttered, fluttered through the pure spring air and flew into Natalie's tender heart—*a need to love, to love, to love!!!* This is the entire riddle; this is the reason for the beauty's sadness—and if it appears not quite comprehensible to any one of my readers, then let him demand a more detailed explanation from the eighteen-year-old maid who is dearest to him.

From this time Natalie changed in many ways—she was not so lively, she was not so frisky—sometimes she became pensive—even though she walked in the garden and field as in the past, even though she spent her evenings with her girl friends as in the past, she could find in nothing her previous pleasure. So the man, emerging from the years of his childhood, sees the toys which formed his amusement in his infancy —he takes them, wants to play but, feeling that they no longer can divert him, leaves them with a sigh.—Our beauty was not able to explain to herself her new, confused, vague feelings. Her imagination brought forth miracles. For example, often it seemed to her (not only in her dreams but even in waking hours) that in the shimmering of a distant glow, some sort of image drifted before her, a charming, sweet apparition, which beckoned to her with an angelic smile and then disappeared in air. "Ah!" exclaimed Natalie and her outstretched hands slowly dropped down. Sometimes an enormous temple appeared to her inflamed mind, thousands of people, men and women, hurried into it with joyous faces, holding each other by the hand. Natalie also wanted to enter it but an unseen hand grasped her clothing and an unknown voice said to her:

"Stop in the vestibule of the temple; no one can enter inside without a sweet friend." She did not understand the agitation of her heart, she did not know how to interpret her dreams, she did not comprehend what she desired, but strongly felt some sort of deficiency in her soul and pined away. So, beauties! your life in certain years cannot be happy if it flows like a lonely river in a wilderness, and without a sweet shepherd the whole world is a wilderness for you and the merry voices of your girl friends, the merry voices of little birds will seem sad echoes of your lonely boredom. Vainly deceiving your own selves, you want to fill the emptiness of your soul with the feeling of maidenly friendship, vainly you choose the best of your girl friends as the object of tender impulses of your heart! No, beauties, no! Your heart desires something else: it wants a heart which cannot be approached except with strong palpitations, which can form with it one feeling, tender, passionate, ardent—and where can you find it, where? Of course, not in Daphne, of course, not in Chloë, who can only grieve with you, secretly or openly—grieve and mourn, desiring and not finding that which you yourself seek and do not find in a cold friendship, but which you will find—or, if such is not the case, all your life will be a restless, burdensome dream—you will find in the shade of the myrtle arbor, when now there sits, despondent, longing, a sweet youth with light-blue or dark eyes and in sad songs complains of your apparent cruelty.— Dear reader! Forgive me this digression! Not only Sterne was the slave of his pen.—Let us return again to our tale.

Boyar Matvei soon observed that Natalie had become gloomier: his parental heart was bothered. He inquired with tender solicitude the reason for such a change and, finally, concluding that his daughter was ill, he sent a special courier to his hundred-year-old aunt, who lived deep in the Murom Woods, collected grasses and roots, mixed more with the wolves and bears than with Russian people, and was reputed to be if not a sorceress, then at least a very wise old woman, skillful in treating all human ailments. Boyar Matvei described all the symptoms of Natalie's illness and implored her to restore the health of her grandniece by means of her art and restore to him, an old man, joy and serenity. The success of this embassy remains obscure; on the other hand there is no great need even to know it. Now we must proceed to the description of the most important adventures.

Time flew just as quickly in the old days as it does today, and, while our beauty sighed and pined away, the year revolved on its axis: the green carpets of spring and summer were covered with a powdery snow, the terrible tsaritsa of the cold ascended her icy throne and breathed snowstorms upon the Russian kingdom, that is, winter came, and Natalie as was her custom went one day to mass. Having prayed zealously, she unintentionally turned her eyes toward the left chancel—and what did she see? A handsome young man, in a light-blue caftan with gold buttons, stood there as a tsar among all the rest, and his glittering, penetrating gaze met her gaze. Natalie in a second blushed and her heart, beginning to palpitate strongly, said to her: "It is he! . . ." She lowered her eyes but not for long; again she glanced at the handsome man, again her face flushed, and again her heart began to palpitate. It seemed to her that the beloved apparition, which night and day enticed her imagination, was none other than the image of this young man,—and for this reason she looked at him as on a sweet acquaintance. A new light began to shine in her soul as if it had been awakened by the appearance of the sun, but it was still not fully conscious after the many disconnected, entangled fantasies which had agitated it during the long night. "So," thought Natalie, "so, there really is in this world such a sweet handsome man, such a man—such a charming youth? What a figure! What a bearing! What a white, glowing face! And the eyes, his eyes are like lightning; I, timid, am

afraid to glance at them. He looks at me, looks so intently—
and even then while he is praying. Of course, I am also known
to him; perhaps he also, like me, was sad, sighed, thought,
thought—and saw me—although darkly, nonetheless he saw
me just as I saw him in my soul."

The reader ought to realize that the ideas of beautiful
maidens are usually very rapid when there begins to stir in
their hearts that which they cannot for a long time call by
name and which at these moments Natalie felt. The mass
seemed quite short to her. The nurse tugged her by the figured
jacket ten times and ten times said to her: "Let's go, young
lady; everything has ended." But the young lady still had not
moved from the spot, because the handsome stranger stood as
if transfixed beside the left chancel. They watched each other
and sighed very quietly. The old nanny, since her eyesight was
poor, did not see anything and thought that Natalie was
praying silently and therefore did not leave the church. Finally, the sexton began to rattle his keys: the beauty collected
her senses and, realizing that the church was to be locked,
walked toward the doors, with the young man behind her—
she on the left, he on the right. Natalie stumbled once or
twice, once or twice she dropped her handkerchief and had to
turn back; the stranger adjusted his belt, stood on the same
spot, looking—at the beauty and still did not put on his
beaver cap, although it was cold outside.

Natalie returned home and thought of nothing but the
young man in the light-blue caftan with the golden buttons.
She was not sad, nor for that matter happy, like a person who
recognizes finally where his bliss lies but has only a small hope
of enjoying it. At dinner she did not eat, a custom of all those
who are in love—but why not tell us directly and simply
that she had fallen in love with the stranger? "In one minute?" the reader will say.—"Having seen him for the first
time and never having heard a word from him?" Dear sirs! I

am relating how this affair took place: do not doubt its truth; do not doubt the strength of that mutual inclination which two hearts, created one for the other, feel! But he who does not believe in sympathy, be gone from us and read not our history, which is meant only for those sensitive souls who possess this sweet faith!

When Boyar Matvei dozed off after dinner (not on the Voltairean armchairs on which our boyars sleep today, but on a broad, oak bench), Natalie went with her nurse into her room, sat beneath her beloved window, took from her pocket a white handkerchief, wanted to say something, but thought better of it—glanced at the window edges, with their frosty designs—adjusted the pearl fillet on her head, and then, looking at her knees, asked her nurse in a low and slightly quivering voice what she thought of the young man who had been at mass. The old woman did not understand of whom she was speaking. It was necessary to explain, but was this easy for a bashful maiden? "I speak of him," Natalie continued, "of him, who—who is the finest of all." The nurse still did not understand and the beauty was forced to say that he had stood beside the left chancel and had left the church behind them. "I did not notice him," the old woman answered coldly, and Natalie very quietly shrugged her beautiful little shoulders in amazement at how it was possible not to notice him!

The next day Natalie arrived earlier than anyone else at mass and left the church later than anyone else, but the handsome man in the light-blue caftan was not there—he was not there on the third day, and the sensitive boyar's daughter did not want to drink or eat, she ceased sleeping and was hardly able to walk, but she tried to hide her inner torment from her parent and also from her nurse. Only at night did her tears flow onto the soft pillow. "Cruel one," she thought, "cruel one! Why do you conceal yourself from my eyes, which seek you every moment? Do you really want my early death?

I shall die, I shall die—and you will not shed a small tear on the grave of an ill-fated girl!" Ah! why is the most tender, most ardent of the passions born always with woe, since what lover does not sigh, what lover is not full of longing in the first days of his passion, believing that he is not loved reciprocally.

The fourth day Natalie again went to mass, despite her weakness, the cruel frost, the fact that the Boyar Matvei, having perceived the unusual pallor of her face the evening before, implored her to take care of herself and not go outside during cold weather. No one was yet in the church. The beauty, standing in her place, looked at the doors. The first man entered—it was not he! The second entered—it was not he! The third, the fourth—none of them was he! The fifth entered, and all the little veins stirred in Natalie—it was he, that handsome man whose image had been forever impressed in her soul! She almost collapsed because of the strong inner agitation and had to lean on the shoulder of her nurse. The stranger bowed to everyone, and especially to her, and, furthermore, far lower and more respectfully than to the others. A languid pallor was apparent on his face, but his eyes shone even more brightly than before; he looked almost continually at the charming Natalie (who because of her tender feelings was even more charming) and sighed so openly that she noticed the heaving of his chest and, regardless of her modesty, guessed the reason. Love, inspired by hope, crimsoned at this moment the cheeks of our sweet beauty, love shone in her glances, love beat in her heart, love raised her hand when she crossed herself. The hour of the mass was a blissful second for her. Everyone began to leave the church; she left after everyone else, but the young man was with her. Instead of going again to the other side, he now walked behind Natalie, who stole a glance at him now over her right and now over her left shoulder. A wondrous thing! Lovers are not able to look enough at each other, like a greedy miser who is never able to get enough gold. At the gates of the Boyar's house, Natalie glanced at the handsome man for the last time and with a tender look said to him: "Farewell, sweet stranger!" The gate slammed and Natalie heard the young man sigh; at least she herself sighed.—The old nurse was more perceptive this time and, without even waiting for a word from Natalie, began to speak of the handsome stranger who accompanied them from church. She praised him with great warmth, she pointed out that he resembled her late son, she did not doubt his aristocratic origin and wished that her young lady would find such a consort. Natalie was glad, blushed, became pensive, answered: "Yes!" "No!" and she did not know herself what she was saying.

On the second day, on the third day she again went to mass, she saw whom she desired to see—she returned home and at the gate said with a tender look: "Farewell!" But the heart of a beautiful maiden is an amazing thing: that which satisfies it today does not satisfy it tomorrow—it always desires more and more and there is no end to its desires. Thus, it was not enough for Natalie to look at the handsome stranger and see the tenderness in his eyes; she wanted to hear his voice, take him by the hand, be nearer to his heart, and so on. What is to be done? How is it to be done? Such desires are difficult to uproot and when they are not fulfilled, a beauty is always sad. Natalie again began to cry. Fate, fate! Will you not really take pity on her? Do you really want these bright eyes to grow dull with tears?—Let us see what will happen.

Once toward evening when the Boyar Matvei was not at home, Natalie saw through the window that their gate had opened—the man in the light-blue caftan entered and the work fell from Natalie's hand—because this man was the handsome stranger. "Nurse!" she said in a weak voice, "who is it?" The nurse looked, smiled, and went out.

"He is here! The nurse grinned, she has gone to him, truly, to him—ah, my God! What will happen?"—Natalie thought, looked out the window, and saw that the young man had already entered the anteroom. Her heart flew to meet him but her shyness said to her: "Stay!" The beauty obeyed this last voice only with agonizing restraint, with great longing, because it is most unbearable of all to oppose the inclination of your heart. She arose, walked about, took up one thing after another, and a quarter of an hour seemed a year to her. Finally the door opened and the creaking shook Natalie's soul. The nurse entered—glanced at the young lady, smiled, and—said not a word. The beauty also did not speak and only with a shy glance asked: "What, Nurse? What?" The old woman seemed to enjoy her confusion, her impatience—she was silent for a while and after several minutes had passed said to her: "Do you know, young lady, that this young man is ill?"—"Ill? Of what?" asked Natalie, and the color of her face changed. —"Very ill," continued the nurse. "His heart is so ill that the poor man can neither drink, nor eat, he is pale as a sheet and can hardly walk. He has been told that I have the medicine for the illness, and for that reason he found his way to me, he weeps bitter tears and implores me to help him. Will you believe, young lady, that tears welled up in my eyes? Such a pity!"—"What else, Nurse? Have you given him the medicine?"—"No, I ordered him to wait a bit."—"Wait a bit? Where?" "In our anteroom." "Is it possible? It is extremely cold there; there are drafts from all sides and he is ill!"— "What can I do then? We have such fumes downstairs that he might be poisoned, where can he go while I prepare the medicine? Is it possible here? Is it possible to direct him to enter the living quarters? This will be a fine thing, young lady; he is an honorable man—he will pray to God for you and never forget your mercy. Right now your sire is not at home—it is dusk, dark—no one will see and there will be no harm; really only in fairy tales are men usually terrible to beautiful maidens! What do you think, madame?" Natalie (I do not know why) trembled and in a hesitant voice answered her: "I think . . . as you wish . . . you know better than I." Here the nurse opened the door—and the young man threw himself at Natalie's feet. The beauty gasped, and her eyes closed for a moment; her white hands hung down and her head bent to her high bosom. The stranger dared to kiss her hand, again, a third time—he dared to kiss the beauty's rosy lips, again, a third time, and with such fervor that the nanny was frightened and cried out: "Sir! Sir! Remember our agreement!" Natalie opened her dark eyes, which immediately met the dark eyes of the stranger, because they were close to each other at this moment; and ardent feelings, a heart burning with love, were depicted both in his and her eyes. Natalie was able with difficulty to raise her head a bit so that she might relieve her bosom with a sigh. Then the young man began to speak—not in the language of novels but in the language of real sensitivity; he said in simple, tender, passionate words that he had caught sight of her and fallen in love, fallen so in love that he could not be happy and did not want to live without her reciprocal love. The beauty was silent; only her heart and glances spoke—but the mistrustful stranger still desired verbal confirmation and, on his knees, he asked her: "Natalie, beautiful Natalie! Do you love me? Your answer will decide my fate: I can be the happiest man on earth or the murmuring Moscow River will be my grave."—"Ah, young lady!" said the pitying nurse. "Tell him quickly that you like him! Do you want, really, to destroy his soul?"—"You are dear to my heart," Natalie uttered in a tender voice, placing her hand on his shoulder. "May God grant," she added, raising her eyes to the heavens and again turning to the delighted stranger, "may God grant that I be just as dear to you!" They embraced; their breathing seemed to stop. He who has seen how chaste lovers embrace, how a virtuous maiden for the first time kisses her dear friend, forgetting for the first time her maidenly bashfulness, let him then imagine this picture; I do not dare describe it—but it was touching—the old nurse herself, a witness of this scene, shed some two teardrops and forgot to remind the lover of their agreement, but the goddess of virtue was there unseen in Natalie's living quarters.

After the first minute of mute rapture the young man, looking at the beauty, was drowned in tears. "You are weeping?" said Natalie in a tender voice, her head bent on his shoulder. "Ah! I must open my heart to you, charming Natalie!"† he answered. "It still is not completely convinced of its happiness."—"What does it still need?" asked Natalie and impatiently awaited the answer. "Promise that you will fulfill my demand."—"Tell me, tell me, what is it? I shall fulfill it, I shall do everything that you command."—"This night, after the moon has descended—at the time when the first cocks crow, I shall come in a sled to your gate, you must come out and go with me; this is what I demand of you!"— "Go? This night? Where?"—"First to the church where we are to be wed, and then to where I live."—"How can this be? Without my father's knowledge? Without his blessing?"— "Without his knowledge, without his blessing, or I am lost!" "My God! My heart has stopped. To go away secretly from my parental home? What then will happen to my sire? He will die of grief and a terrible sin will rest on my soul. Sweet friend! Why don't we throw ourselves at his feet? He will love you, bless you, and he himself will allow us to marry."— "We shall throw ourselves at his feet a little later. Now he cannot agree to our marriage. My very life would be in danger

† The reader has guessed that lovers of old did not speak as they do now; but now we would not be able to understand the language of that day. It is only necessary to suggest it in a *certain fashion* by using the *coloration of ancient times.*

if I am recognized."—"If you are recognized? You, the sweet one of my soul? My God! How evil people are, if you speak the truth! Only I cannot believe it. Tell me, what is your name?" "Aleksei."—"Aleksei? I have always loved that name. What harm is there if you are recognized?" "Everything will be known to you if you agree to make me happy. Charming, sweet Natalie! Time is passing, I cannot remain longer with you. That your parent, whom I myself love and respect for his good deeds—that your parent should not be overwhelmed and should not consider his daughter lost, I shall write a letter and inform him that you are alive and that he can soon see you. Tell me, tell me, what do you want: my life or death?" With these words, pronounced in a firm voice, he got up and looked at the beauty with fiery, ardent eyes.—"You are asking me?" she said sensitively. "Have I not promised to obey you? From very infancy I have been accustomed to love my parent, because he also loves me, he loves me very, very much." (Here Natalie with a handkerchief wiped away her tears, which fell one after the other from her eyes.) "I have not known you for long but I love you even more: how this has happened, I do not know."—Aleksei embraced her with a new delight, took a golden ring from his finger, put it on Natalie's, said: "You are mine!" and disappeared like lightning. The old woman, the nurse, conducted him out.

We as well as our reader truly reprove Natalie, truly censure her because she, having seen the young man some three times and having heard several pleasant words from him, suddenly decided to flee with him from her parental home, not knowing where—to entrust her fate to an unknown man, whom, from his own statements, one could consider suspicious —but what is more important—to leave a good, sensitive, tender father. . . . But such is a terrible love! It can make a criminal of the most virtuous man. And he who has loved ardently in his life, and has in no wise violated a strict moral code, he—is happy. Happy in that his passion was not opposed to virtue—otherwise the latter would have acknowledged its weakness and tears of vain repentance would have flowed like a river. The chronicles of the human heart convince us of this sad truth.

In regard to the nurse, the young man (after he had seen Natalie in church) found a way to discuss the affair with her and to bring her to his side by various lavish promises and gifts. Alas! People, and especially toward old age, are usually susceptible to silver and gold. The old woman had forgotten that she, for more than forty years, had served blamelessly and faithfully in the house of Boyar Matvei—she had forgotten and sold herself to a stranger. But then, a shard of honesty remaining, she got his promise to marry the beautiful Natalie and until that time not to misuse her love and innocence.

Natalie, after her lover had left, stood motionless for several moments; signs of strong spiritual agitation were evident on her face but no doubt, no wavering—for she had already decided! And while a small voice from the depths of her heart, as if from a distant cavern, asked her: "What are you doing, reckless girl?" another voice, in that very same heart, far more powerful, answered for her: "I am in love!"

The nurse returned and tried to calm Natalie, telling her that she would be the spouse of a handsome young man and that a wife, by the very law, must leave everything and forget everything for her husband.—"Forget?" Natalie interrupted, catching the last words. "No! I shall remember my parent, I shall pray for him every day. Furthermore, he told me that we will, soon, throw ourselves at my sire's feet—isn't it so, Nurse?"—"Of course, young lady," the old woman answered. "That which he said will happen, will."—"True, it will!" said Natalie, and her face became gayer.

The Boyar Matvei returned home late and, thinking that his daughter was already sleeping, did not drop in upon her in her living quarters. Midnight approached.—Natalie thought not about sleep but about her sweet friend, to whom she had given her heart forever and whom she impatiently awaited. The moon still shone in the heavens—the moon, which before had been a delight to her eyes, now became unpleasant to her; now the beauty thought: "How slowly you roll through the circular heavens! Descend more quickly, bright moon! He, he will come for me when you have vanished!"—The moon was setting—a portion of it had already descended behind the horizon—the darkness in the air had thickened—the cocks had begun to crow—the moon disappeared—a silver ring tinkled at the Boyar's gate. Natalie started. "Ah, Nurse! Run, run quickly; he has come!" In a moment the young man appeared and Natalie threw herself into his embrace. "Here's the letter for your parent," he said, showing a paper.— "The letter to my parent? Ah! Read it! I want to hear what you have written." The young man unfolded the paper and read the following lines: "I love your dear daughter more than anything else in the world—you could not consent to allow her to marry me—she is going with me—forgive us!—Love is always stronger—perhaps, in time, I shall be worthy to be called your son-in-law."—Natalie took the letter and, although she did not know how to read, nonetheless looked at it, and tears poured from her eyes. "Write," said she, "write some more, that I implore him not to weep, not to mourn, and that the paper is wet with my tears; write that I myself am not free and that he should either forget or forgive me."

The young man took pen and inkhorn from his pocket—he wrote what Natalie had said and left the letter on the table. Then the beauty, having put on her fox fur coat, prayed to God, took the icon which her late mother had blessed, and having given her hand to the happy lover, left her living quarters, descended the tall porch, and went out into the court —she glanced at her parental home, wiped away the last tears, sat in the sleigh, pressed herself to her sweet one, and said: "Take me where you wish!" The coachman whipped the horses and the horses started to dash off when suddenly a plaintive voice resounded: "They are abandoning me, poor, unhappy me!" The young man glanced back and saw the running nurse, who had remained for a minute in the room to put away several of Natalie's precious things, and whom our lovers were on the point of forgetting. The horses were reined up, the old woman was seated, again they galloped off, and in a quarter of an hour had left Moscow. On the right side of the road, in the distance, a small light shone; they turned there, and Natalie saw a lowish, wooden church, piled up with snow. Aleksei (the reader has not forgotten the name of the young man)—Aleksei led his love into this dilapidated temple which was illuminated by a small, weakly burning icon lamp. An old priest, bent by the weight of his years, met them there, and, in a trembling voice, said to them: "I have waited a long time for you, dear children! My grandson has already dozed off." He awakened the lad, sleeping in the corner of the church, stood the lovers before the lectern, and began to wed them. The lad read, sang what was required, looked in astonishment at the bridegroom and bride, and trembled at every gust of wind which noised through the broken windows of the church. Aleksei and Natalie prayed zealously, and, pronouncing their vows, looked at each other with tender emotion and sweet tears. On completing the ceremony the very old priest said to the newlyweds: "I do not know and do not ask who you are but in the name of the great God, of whom both the dark of night and the noise of the storm speak (at this instant the wind began to blow fearfully)—in the name of the incomprehensible, terrible to the evildoers, merciful to the good, I promise you well-being in life, if you will always love each other, because conjugal love is a holy love, pleasing to the Deity, and he who maintains it in a pure heart—it cannot live in the impure—is pleasing to the Most High. Go in peace and remember my words!" The newlyweds received the blessing from the elder, kissed his hand, kissed each other, left the church, and drove on.

The wind piled the snow on the road but the frisky steeds flew on, like lightning—their nostrils smoked, the steam curled up in a column, and the powdery snow rose from their hooves like clouds. Soon our travelers drove into the dark of the woods, where there was not even a road. The old woman, the nurse, trembled in fear, but the beautiful Natalie, feeling her sweet friend beside her, feared nothing. The young consort pushed aside with his hand all the twigs and branches which threatened to pierce the white face of his spouse. He held her in his embrace when the sleigh sank deep in the snowdrifts, and with his fervent kisses he removed the cold from the tender roses which blossomed on her lips. For about four hours they drove through the woods, making their way through rows of tall trees. The horses had begun to tire and dragged their legs with difficulty out of the snowy depths; the sleigh moved slowly, and finally Natalie, clasping the hand of her dear one, asked him in a low voice: "Shall we soon arrive?" Aleksei looked about him, at the crowns of the trees, and said that his dwelling was not far. Actually, after several minutes they drove out onto a narrow plain, where there stood a small house, enclosed by a tall fence. Five or six men with bunches of burning brands and armed with long knives, which hung from their belts, emerged to meet them. The old woman, the nurse, seeing the wild, solitary dwelling in the midst of an impassable woods, seeing these armed servants and observing in their faces something sullen and ferocious, was terrified, threw up her hands, and cried: "Alas! We are lost! We are in the hands—of brigands!"

Here I could depict a terrifying picture to the eyes of the readers—tempted innocence, deceived love, an unhappy beauty in the power of barbarians, murderers, a wife of the ataman of the brigands, a witness of terrible villainies, and finally, after an agonizing life, expiring on the scaffold beneath a poleax of justice, before the eyes of an unhappy parent; I could depict all these events as probable, natural, and the sensitive man would shed tears of woe and sorrow— but in such a case I would have departed from historical truth, on which my narrative is based. No, dear reader, no! This time spare your tears—be calm—the old woman, the nurse, was mistaken—Natalie is not among brigands.

Natalie is not among brigands! . . . But who then is the mysterious young man, or, to speak in the language of Ossian, the *son of danger and darkness,* living in the depths of the forest?—I beg you to read further.

Natalie became uneasy at the exclamation of the nurse, grabbed Aleksei by the hand, and, looking into his eyes with some anxiety but with complete confidence in the beloved of her soul, asked: "Where are we?" The young man glanced angrily at the old woman, then, fixing a tender gaze on his sweet Natalie, answered with a smile: "You are among good people—don't be afraid." Natalie grew calm because he whom she loved ordered her to be calm!

They entered the house, which was divided into two halves. "Here my servants live," said Aleksei, pointing to the right. "And here—I." In the first chamber there hung swords and halberds, spike helmets and coats of mail, while in the other there stood a high bed, and before the icon of the Virgin Mary there burned an icon lamp. Natalie placed her icon right there, prayed, and, glancing sweetly at Aleksei, bowed low to him as to the master of the house. The young consort took the fox fur coat from the beauty, warmed her hands with his breath, sat her down on the oak bench, looked at the charmer, and wept from joy. Sweet Natalie wept with him because tenderness and happiness also have their own tears. . . .

The young beauty forgot her curiosity or, better, she had none at all, since she knew that the one sweet to her soul could not be an evil man. Ah! If all people, as many as there were then in the Russian kingdom, would have said in unison to Natalie: "Aleksei is a villain!" she with a quiet smile would have answered them: "No! . . . my heart knows him better than you; my heart says that he is dearest of all, best of all. I will not listen to you."

But Aleksei himself began to speak. "Dear Natalie!"— said he, "the mystery of my life must be revealed to you. The will of the Most High has joined us forever; nothing can ever sunder our union. A consort must hide nothing from his spouse. Therefore, know that I am the son of the unhappy Boyar Liuboslavskii."—"Liuboslavskii? Is it possible? My sire told me that he disappeared without a trace."—"He is no longer in the world. Hear me out.—You do not remember but, of course, have heard of those disturbances and insurrections which some thirty years ago upset the tranquillity of our kingdom. Several of the most aristocratic, ambitious boyars rose up against the legal power of the young sovereign, but soon a divine wrath punished the insurgents—their innumerable accomplices were dispersed, like dust, and the blood of the chief insurrectionists was shed at the executioner's block. My parent was taken into custody because of a certain, completely false, suspicion. He had enemies, evil and crafty; they presented evidence of his purported treason and consentience with the insurgents; my father swore to his innocence, but circumstances convicted him and the hand of the supreme judge was prepared to sign his death warrant—hope was disappearing in the soul of the innocent one—only the Most High could save him—and He saved him. A devoted friend opened the door of the dungeon—and my parent vanished, taking with him his most zealous servants and me, his twelve-year-old son. There was no safety for us within the confines of

Russia: we withdrew to that land where the River Sviiaga flows into the majestic Volga and where innumerable people worship the false prophet Mahomet—a superstitious people but lovers of strangers. They accepted us as friends and we lived with them for some ten years; we lacked nothing but incessantly grieved for our fatherland; we sat on the high bank of the Volga and, looking at her waves, borne from the Russian lands, we shed fervent tears; every bird which flew from the west † seemed sweeter to us; every bird which flew to the west we accompanied with our eyes and—our sighs.—Meanwhile, my father annually sent a secret courier to Moscow and received letters from his friend, which always gave hope that our innocence sooner or later would be revealed and that we would be able to return to our fatherland with honor. But sorrow desiccated the heart of my parent, his strength was disappearing, and his eyes were being veiled by heavy darkness. Without terror he felt the approach of his end—he blessed me—and, having said: 'God and our friend will not abandon you,' died in my embrace. I shall not speak of the woe of a poor orphan; my eyes were not dry for several months.—I informed our friend of my misfortune; in his reply, which expressed his sincere sorrow at the demise of the innocent sufferer, who died in a land of strangers and was buried in non-Christian earth, this beneficent friend summoned me to Russia. 'Some forty versts from Moscow,' he wrote, 'in a dense, impassable woods, I have built a solitary little house known to no one except me and my trustworthy servants. There you will live in complete safety until the proper time. The messenger knows the place.'—I expressed my thanks to the hospitable inhabitants of the Volga banks, took leave of the green grave of my parent, kissed and watered with my tears every little flower, every little blade of grass,

† That is, from Russia.

growing on it, returned with my devoted servants to the confines of Russia, kissed the earth of the fatherland—and in the depths of the dark woods, on this narrow plain, I found this uninhabited little house, where you are with me now, dear Natalie. A gray-haired old man met me here and said in a trembling voice: 'You are the son of Boyar Liuboslavskii! My master, his devoted friend, who wanted to be your second father and built this dwelling for you—has passed away! But he remembered the orphan at his demise. Here you will find all the necessities of life; you will find treasures: they are yours.'—I raised my eyes to the heavens; I was silent—and my tears rolled forth in a deluge. 'Who will be my helper?' I thought. 'My mentor? I am alone in the world! . . . Most High! You to whom my parent entrusted me! Do not abandon this poor being!'

"I settled down in these wilds; I saw that I had much silver and gold, but was not in the least consoled by it. After several days I felt like visiting the sovereign city, where no one was able to recognize me. The old attendant of my benefactor indicated to me different marks on the trees which led to the Moscow highway and which were incomprehensible to anyone but us. I saw the glittering domes of the churches, the multitude of people, enormous houses, all the wonders of a great town, and joyful tears sparkled in my eyes. The golden days of childhood, days of innocence and amusement, which I had passed in the Russian capital, appeared to my mind as a happy fantasy. I sought out our former house and found only desolate walls, where bats fluttered about. . . . —A cold terror spread through my insides.

"Afterward I often visited Moscow, stopping in a quiet inn and calling myself a merchant from another town, often I saw the Sovereign, the father of the people, often I heard of the good deeds of your parent, when the boyars, gathering in the square opposite the cathedral church, related to each other all his good and praiseworthy deeds which were the capital's adornment. Returning to these wilds, I fought with the wild beasts, which we had to destroy for our own safety, but soon, letting the booty fall from my hands, I fell to the earth and shed tears. Sadness came to me everywhere—in the desolate woods and amidst people. Grief-laden, I walked the streets of the sovereign city and, looking at the people whom I met, I thought: They are going to their families and friends, who are waiting for them, who will be happy to see them—I have no one to go to, no one is waiting for me, no one thinks about an orphan! Sometimes I wanted to throw myself at the feet of the Sovereign, assure him of the innocence of my father, of my loyalty to the God-fearing Tsar, and entrust my fate to his mercy; but some sort of powerful unseen hand did not allow me to carry out this intention.

"Gloomy autumn came, boring winter came; the woody solitude became even more unendurable for me. More often than before I began to go into town and—I saw you, beautiful Natalie. You seemed a divine angel to me. . . . No! It is said that the radiance of angels blinds human eyes and that it is impossible to look at them for long, but I want to gaze incessantly upon you. I have seen many beauties before, marveled at their charms, and often thought, The Lord God has created nothing better than the beautiful Moscow maidens, but my eyes looked at them and my heart was silent and unmoved—they seemed *strangers* to me. With your first glance you instilled some sort of fire in my heart, with your first glance you gained my soul, which immediately loved you as *its own*. I wanted to rush forward and press you so tightly to my breast that nothing could ever separate us again.—You left, and it seemed to me that the beautiful sun had set and night had come. I stood on the street and did not feel the snow, which fell heavily on me; finally I came to my senses—made inquiries and, finding out who you were, returned to my

inn and reflected upon the sweet daughter of Boyar Matvei.
My sire had often spoken to me of the love which he felt for
my mother upon seeing her for the first time and which gave
him no rest until they were led to church. The same thing is
happening to me, I thought, and I can be neither peaceful nor
happy without sweet Natalie. But how could I hope? Would
the favorite boyar of the Tsar want to give his daughter in
marriage to a man whose father was considered a criminal? It
is true, if she loved me . . . even the wilds with her would be
better than white-stoned Moscow. Perhaps I am wrong—only
it seemed to me that she looked sympathetically at me. . . .
But I, of course, am wrong. How could this be? Such happiness does not come suddenly! Night came—and passed, but
my eyes were not closed by sleep. You were continually before
me or in my soul—you crossed yourself with a white hand and
concealed it beneath your sable jacket.—The next day I experienced a strong headache and a very great weakness, which
confined me for two days to my bed." "So," Natalie broke in,
"so! I knew it; my heart yearned not without reason. You
were not at mass either on the second or the third day."

"However, even the illness did not prevent me from thinking about you. One of my servants was at the home of your
parent, met your nurse, and persuaded her to visit me at the
inn. I revealed my love to the old woman, implored, beseeched, assured her of my gratitude—finally she agreed to
help me.—You know the rest. I saw you in church—sometimes I flattered myself that I was loved, observing in your
eyes a tender sweetness and a blush on your face when our
glances met—finally I decided to find out my fate—I fell at
your feet, and the poor orphan became the happiest man in
the world. Could I have parted with you after your avowal?
Could I live beneath another roof and worry every hour and
think every hour: Is she alive? Do not some dangers threaten
her? Is not her heart yearning? Ah! Would not some suitor,

rich and aristocratic, be betrothed to the beauty?—No, no! I would die or live with you! The priest of the outlying church, who wed us, had not been bribed but had been prevailed upon by me: my tears touched the elder.

"Now you know who your consort is; now all my desires have been fulfilled. Sadness, boredom! Farewell! There is no place in my solitary little house for you. Sweet Natalie loves me, sweet Natalie is with me!—But I see a languor in your eyes, you must be calm, dear one of my soul. The night will pass and soon the morning glow will appear in the heavens."

Aleksei kissed Natalie's hand. The beauty sighed. "Ah! Why isn't my sire with us!" she said, pressing her consort to her heart. "When shall we see him? When will he bless us? When shall I kiss you in his presence, friend of my heart?"— "That," answered Aleksei, "that kind God, Who gave you to me, will in truth do everything for us. Let us trust in Him: He will send the opportunity for us to fall at the feet of your parent and accept his blessing."

Having said these words, he arose and walked into the front chamber. His servants sat there with the nurse, who (convinced that they were not brigands and that the long knives served only as a defense against the woodland beasts) had ceased being afraid, had become acquainted with them, and with the curiosity of an old woman was inquiring about their young master, of the reason for his hermitlike existence, and so on, and so on. Aleksei whispered into the ear of one man and in a minute no one was in the chamber: they seized the old woman by the arm and led her into the other half. The young consort returned to his beloved—helped her undress— their hearts were beating—he took her by the white hand. . . . But my modest muse covers her face with a white handkerchief—not a word! The sacred curtain descends, sacred and impenetrable to curious eyes!

But you, happy nuptial pair, be blessed in your passionate

delights under the influence of the heavenly stars, but be chaste in the supreme delights of your passion. Let an innocent modesty live inseparably with you—and the tender flowers of pleasure will never wilt on your conjugal bed!

The sun had already risen high in the heavens and scattered millions of its glittering diamonds over the snow while in the bedroom of our nuptial pair a deep silence still continued to reign. The old woman, the nanny, had long since risen, had approached the door some ten times, listened and heard nothing; finally she took it into her head to knock quietly and said rather loudly: "It's time to get up—it's time to get up!" After several minutes the door was unlocked. Aleksei was already in his light-blue caftan, but the beauty was still lying in the bed and for a long time could not look at the old woman, being ashamed—for some unknown reason. The roses on her cheeks had paled somewhat, a languid weakness was expressed in her eyes—but Natalie had never been so alluring as on this morning. She dressed with her nurse's help, prayed tearfully to God, and waited for her consort, who in the meantime was busy with the household affairs, ordering the preparation of the dinner and other things necessary for domestic life. When he returned to his dear spouse, she embraced him tenderly and said in a low voice: "Sweet friend! I am thinking of my sire—Ah! He, in truth, is yearning, weeping, grieving for me! I would like to hear something about him, I would like to know . . ."—Natalie did not finish her sentence, but Aleksei understood her wish and immediately dispatched a man to Moscow to find out about Boyar Matvei.

But we shall anticipate this messenger and look at what is happening in the sovereign city.—Boyar Matvei had long been waiting the early morning visit of his sweet Natalie and finally went to her living quarters. There everything was deserted, everything was in disorder. He was dumfounded—he saw a letter on the small table, unfolded it, read through

it—did not believe his eyes—read it through again—still did
not want to believe it—but his trembling legs bent under him
—he fell to the floor. He was unconscious for several minutes.
Having regained consciousness, he ordered his servants to
conduct him to the Sovereign. "Sovereign!" said the old man,
shaking. "Sovereign!" He could not speak and gave Aleksei's
letter to the Tsar. The brow of the God-fearing monarch grew
dark in anger. "Who is this dishonorable seducer?" said he.—
"But the terrible hand of justice will find him wherever he is."
—He spoke and to all the lands of the Russian kingdom
couriers were dispatched with the command to seek out Natalie and her abductor.

The Tsar consoled the Boyar as his friend. Sighs and tears
eased the burden of the constricted breast of the unhappy
parent, and the feeling of anger in his heart gave way to a
tender woe. "God sees," said he, looking at the heavens, "God
sees how I loved you, ungrateful, cruel, sweet Natalie! . . . So,
Sovereign! She even now is sweeter to me than anything else
in the world! Who carried her away from her parental home?
Where is she? What's happening to her? Ah! In the decline of
my days I would pursue her to the edge of the world! . . .
Perhaps some villain has seduced the innocent girl and afterward will discard, destroy her. . . . No! My daughter could
not love a villain! But why not confide in her parent?
Whoever he might be, I would embrace him as a son. Does
not the Sovereign favor me? Would he not favor as well my
son-in-law? I do not know what to think! But she is gone! I
weep; she does not see my tears—I shall die; she will not close
the eyes of her father, who found his life and soul in her! . . .
Of course, without the will of the Most High nothing takes
place; perhaps I deserved punishment at His hands. . . . I
submit without a murmur! I beg one thing of You, O Lord:
Be a kind father to her in whatever land. Let me die in my
woe so long as my daughter be safe! It is impossible that she

did not love me, it is impossible. . . ." (Here Boyar Matvei took the letter and read it through again.)—"You were weeping; this paper is wet with your tears: I shall preserve it by my heart as the last sign of your love.—Ah! If you would return to me even an hour before death. . . . But it is the will of the Most High!—Meanwhile your father, an orphan in his old age, will be the father of the unfortunates and the grief-stricken; embracing them as my children—as your brethren —he will say to them with tears: 'Friends! pray for Natalie.' " So spoke the Boyar Matvei, and the sensitive Tsar was touched to the depths of his heart.

From that day on, good Boyar, your life was veiled in the dark of sadness—alas! even virtue itself cannot preserve us beforehand from woe! You will think continually of the sweet one of your heart—sigh and sit, sunk in grief, before the wide gates of your home! No one, no one will bring you news of the charming Natalie! The Tsar's couriers will return and their sighs will answer your questions. The poor will sit at the table of the Boyar who loves the lowly but his bread will seem bitter to them—for they will see the sorrow on the face of their benefactor!

Meanwhile Aleksei's messenger returned to the wilds with the information that Boyar Matvei was at the Tsar's palace and that the command had been given to search for his missing daughter throughout Russia. Natalie wanted to know more and asked what could be seen on the face of her parent when he was leaving the Sovereign's palace; was he sighing, was he weeping, had he not very quietly uttered her name? The messenger could not answer either *yes* or *no* because even though he saw the Boyar, he had not looked at him with the penetrating eyes of a tender daughter. "Why," said Natalie, "why could I not become invisible or a tiny bird in order to fly away to white-stoned Moscow, look at my parent, kiss his hand, let fall a burning tear on it, and return to my sweet friend?"—"Ah, no! I would not allow you!" answered Aleksei. "Who knows what might happen to you? No, my friend! I cannot even think of parting—and you can!" Natalie felt a tender reproach and excused herself to her consort with a smile, tears, and a kiss.

Now I should describe the happiness of the young nuptial pair, lovers, concealed by the woody darkness from the whole world, but you, who have enjoyed a similar happiness, tell me, can it be described?—Natalie and Aleksei, living in their solitude, never saw how time glided by or flew. The hours and minutes, the days and nights, the weeks and months blended together in their wilderness as the river's streams, inseparable to the human eye. Ah! the pleasures of love are always the same yet always new and numberless. Natalie awoke and—loved; she arose from her bed and—loved; she prayed and—loved; whatever she thought—she loved everything and enjoyed everything.—Aleksei was the same and their feelings were combined in a delightful harmony.

But the reader should not think that in their solitary life they only looked at each other and sat, arms crossed, from morning until evening. No! Natalie took up her handwork, her embroidering, and had quickly embroidered two beautiful towels with various silk threads and various designs: the first for her sweet consort that he might dry his white face with it and the other for her dear parent. "For the day when we visit him!" said the beauty, and sighed very quietly.—In regard to Aleksei, he, sitting beside his spouse, drew various landscapes and small pictures in ink—he admired the ones which pleased Natalie and tried to improve those which seemed incomplete to her. Yes, dear reader! Aleksei knew how to draw and furthermore not badly at all for nature herself had taught him this art. He saw the image of luxuriant trees in the pellucid rivers and attempted to capture this shadow on paper; the effort was successful, and his sketches quickly became true copies of nature: and not only the trees but other subjects as well were sketched with the greatest exactness. The beauty watched the movement of his hand and marveled at how he was able with only the lines of his pen to represent various views: now an oak grove, now the Moscow towers, now the Sovereign's palace.—But Aleksei no more fought the wild beasts for they (as if out of respect for the beautiful Natalie, the new inhabitant of their dense woods) did not approach the dwelling of the nuptial pair and roared only in the distance. In this way winter passed, the snow melted, the rivers and streams began to murmur, the earth was covered with little grasses, and little green tufts blossomed on the trees. Aleksei ran out of his little house, plucked the first little flower, and brought it to Natalie. She smiled, kissed her friend —and at this very moment spring birds began to sing in the woods. "Ah, what joy! What merriment," said the beauty.— "My friend! Let us go for a walk!" They went and sat on the bank of the river. "Do you know," said Natalie to her consort, "do you know that I could not listen to the little birds last spring without sadness? Now it seems as if I understand them and think the same as they. Look: here on the little bush two little birds are singing—apparently robins—look how they embrace with their little wings; they love each other, as I love you, my friend, and as you love me! Isn't it true?" Anyone can imagine Aleksei's answer and the various pleasures which spring brought to our recluses.

But the tender daughter, enjoying her love, did not forget her parent. Aleksei had to send a man to Moscow some two or three times a week to find out about Boyar Matvei. The news brought back was the same: The Boyar carried on his good deeds, grieved, fed the poor and told them: "Friends! Pray for Natalie!" Natalie sighed and looked at the icon.

Once the messenger returned in great haste. "Sir!" he said to Aleksei, "Moscow is in turmoil. The fierce Lithuanians have risen against the Russian kingdom. I saw how the inhabitants of the capital city have gathered before the Sovereign's palace and how Boyar Matvei, in the name of the Orthodox Tsar, encouraged the warriors; I saw how crowds of people threw their caps up, exclaiming in one voice: 'We shall die for our Sovereign-Tsar! We shall die for the fatherland or conquer the Lithuanians!' I saw how the Russian forces formed ranks, how their swords flashed, and their halberds, and their steel lances. Tomorrow they will take the field under the command of their bravest voivodes."—Aleksei's heart began to palpitate, his blood began to boil—he seized the sword of his father from the wall—glanced at his spouse—and the sword fell to the floor—tears appeared in his eyes. Natalie took him by the hand and said not a word.—"Dear Natalie!" said Aleksei after some silence, "do you desire to return to your parent's home?"

NATALIE: "With you, my friend, with you! Ah! I have not dared to speak to you; only it always seemed to me that we are hiding from my sire for no reason. When he sees us, he will be so glad that he will forget everything, and I shall take you and him by the hand, I shall cry for joy and say: 'Here they are; here are those whom I love—now I am perfectly happy!' "

ALEKSEI: "But I must first earn the Tsar's mercy. The opportunity for this is now."

NATALIE: "What sort of opportunity, my friend?"

ALEKSEI: "To go to war, to fight the enemies of the Russian kingdom, and to conquer. The Tsar will see, then, that the Liuboslavskiis love him and serve their fatherland loyally."

NATALIE: "Let us go, my friend. So long as you are with me, I am prepared for everything."

ALEKSEI: "What are you saying, sweet Natalie? Death-dealing arrows fly there, swords cleave there: how can you go with me?"

NATALIE: "Then you want to leave me? You want my death? Because I cannot live without you. Was it long ago, my friend, was it long ago that you said that you would never desert me? And now you want to go alone, and what is worse, there where the arrows fly? . . . Who will protect you? . . . No, you will take me with you—or is poor Natalie no longer dear to your heart?"

Aleksei embraced his spouse. "Let us go," he said. "Let us go and die together, if it please God! Only women are not usually found in war, sweet Natalie!" The beauty thought a bit, smiled, went into the bedroom, and locked the door behind her. After several minutes, a handsome youth came out. Aleksei was astonished but soon recognized in this handsome youth the dear daughter of Boyar Matvei and rushed to kiss her. Natalie was dressed in the clothes of her consort, which he had worn when he was thirteen or fourteen years old. "I am your younger brother," she said with a wry smile, "now let me have a sharp sword and a steel lance, a spiked helmet, a coat of mail, and an iron shield—you will see that I am no worse than a man." Aleksei was overjoyed with his dear hero, chose for him the lightest weapons, attired him in a coat of mail made of copper links (on which was inscribed: "God is with us: no one shall attack us!" †), armed his own servants, who were prepared to die for their dear master, put on the armor of his late father—and after several hours only Natalie's nanny and two old men remained in the deserted little house.

And we shall leave our nuptial pair for a while in the hope that heaven will not leave them and will be their defense in the dangers that occur where the death-dealing arrows fly, where swords flash like lightning, where lances clash and shatter, where human blood flows like a river, where heroes die for their fatherland and become immortal. Let us return to Moscow—our history started there, and it must end there.

† In the Moscow Armory I saw many coats of mail with this inscription.

Alas! How deserted is the Russian capital! Everything is quiet, everything is sad. No one is to be seen on the streets, except for old weak men and women who with despondent visages go to church to pray to God that He might turn the terrible storm cloud from the Russian kingdom, might bestow victory on the Orthodox warriors, and disperse the Lithuanian hordes. The kindhearted, sensitive Tsar stood on the high porch and impatiently awaited news from the commanders of his forces, which had gone to meet the innumerable foe. Boyar Matvei was inseparable from the God-fearing Tsar. "Sovereign!" said he. "Trust to God and the courage of your subjects, a courage which distinguishes them from all other people. The Russian swords strike terribly; firm as a rock are the breasts of your sons—victory will always be their loyal companion."— Thus spoke the Boyar; he thought of the welfare of the fatherland—and pined for his daughter.

A herald came galloping, bathed in sweat and dust—the Tsar met him halfway down the porch and, with a trembling hand, unfolded a letter from the military commanders. The first word was "Victory!"—"Victory!" he exclaimed in joy. "Victory!" exclaimed the boyars.—"Victory!" the people repeated—and one voice resounded throughout the entire sovereign city: "Victory!" and in every heart there was one feeling: *joy!*

The commanders informed the Sovereign of everything in the greatest detail. The battle was most cruel. The first ranks of the Russian forces, pressed by a countless multitude of Lithuanians, had begun to waver and wanted to retreat before a most powerful foe; but suddenly, like thunder, a voice roared: "We shall die or conquer!" and at that very instant from the Russian ranks a young warrior emerged and, sword in hand, rushed upon the enemy; and the others rushed after him; the entire force moved, and exclaiming "We shall die or conquer!" came down like a tempest on the Lithuanians, who, despite their great numbers, quickly fled and were dispersed. "We cannot," wrote the commanders, "extol enough the true worth of that young warrior, to whom all the honor of victory belongs and who pursued, struck the enemy, and captured their leader with his very own hand. His brother, a handsome youth, followed him everywhere, and covered him with his own shield. He did not want to reveal his name to anyone but you, Sovereign. The defeated Lithuanians are fleeing the confines of Russia, and soon your forces will return with glory to the town of Moscow. We ourselves will present to the Tsar the invincible youth, the savior of the fatherland and a man deserving of all your mercy."

The Tsar impatiently awaited his heroes and rode out to meet them in the field, together with the Boyar Matvei and other functionaries. No one remained in Moscow; the weak old men, forgetting their weakness, hurried out of town to meet their children; spouses and mothers, carrying their infants or leading them by the hand, hurried there also. The first rank of the forces appeared—the second and the third; the varicolored standards fluttered above them. The warriors walked with even strides, their swords unsheathed; in the rear, the cavalry—in the front, the commanders, under a canopy of trophies. They saw the Sovereign, and the exclamation "Victory and greetings to the Russian Tsar!" began to thunder through the air. The voivodes fell on their knees before him. He bade them rise and said with a gracious smile: "I thank you in the name of the fatherland." "Sovereign!" they answered. "We were trying to do our duty! But God bestowed victory on us through the hand of this young warrior." Here the young warrior, who had been standing beside them with downcast gaze, kneeled. "Who are you, courageous youth?" asked the Sovereign, extending his right hand to him. "Your name should be glorified within all the borders of the Russian kingdom." "Sovereign!" answered the youth, "the son of the condemned boyar, Liuboslavskii, who ended his days in a land of aliens, is at your mercy." The Tsar raised his eyes to the heavens. "I thank you, O God," he said, "for having given me the opportunity, if only partially, to efface the injustice and malice of people and to reward a deserving son for the suffering of an innocent father! So, courageous youth! The innocence of your parent has been revealed—unfortunately, too late! Alas! I was then an inexperienced lad, and Boyar Matvei was not yet in my council. Evil boyars had slandered Liuboslavskii; one of them, who ended his own life not long ago, confessed to the iniquity of the denunciations, on which the innocent man was condemned. You see my tears.—Be now a friend of your Tsar, the first after Boyar Matvei!"—"Thus, the memory of my father," said Aleksei, "is free of defamation! . . . But I—I am guilty before you, great Sovereign! I carried away the daughter of Boyar Matvei from her parental home!" The Tsar was amazed. "Where is she now?" he asked impatiently.—But the Boyar had already found his daughter: the beautiful Natalie, in warrior's dress, threw herself into his embrace; the spiked helmet fell from her head, and her light-brown hair spilled over her shoulders. The astonished, delighted parent did not dare to believe in this appearance but the heart of the sensitive old man assured him, through its strong palpitations, that his sweet one had been found. He was hardly able to bear his joy and would have collapsed had not the other boyars supported him. He did not speak for a long time, his head lowered on Natalie's shoulder; finally he called her by name, as if wishing to see whether she would respond —he called her his sweet one, his beautiful one—and at each caressing word a new ray of joy shone on his face, which had been sad for so long! It seemed as though his tongue had to learn to pronounce the long-forgotten names, so slowly did he articulate them. And he repeated them so often! Natalie kissed his hands. "You love me as you did!" she said. "You love me as you did!" and warm streams of tears spoke the rest for her. The entire army remained quiet and silent. The Sovereign was touched to the heart, took Aleksei by the hand and led him to the Boyar. "Here," said Natalie, "here—is my consort! Forgive him, my parent, and love him as you love me!" Boyar Matvei raised his head, looked at Aleksei, and gave him his trembling hand. The young man wanted to throw himself on his knees before him but the old man pressed him to his heart together with his sweet daughter.

TSAR: "They are deserving of each other and will be a comfort in your old age."

"She is my daughter," said Boyar Matvei, his voice breaking. "He is my son. . . . O Lord! Let me die in their embrace."

The old man pressed them to his heart again.

The reader can imagine all the consequences. The old woman, the nurse, was brought to town; Boyar Matvei forgave her, and, summoning the priest who wed Aleksei and Natalie, desired that he again bless them in his presence. The married pair lived happily and enjoyed the special favor of the Tsar. Aleksei rendered important services to the fatherland and the Sovereign, services which are mentioned in different historical manuscripts. The benevolent Boyar Matvei lived to a ripe old age and delighted in his daughter, his son-in-law, and their beautiful children. Death appeared in the guise of his very young and very dear grandson; he wanted to embrace the dear lad—and passed away.—I did not hear anything more from the grandmother of my grandfather, but several years ago, while strolling one autumn along the banks of the Moscow River, near a dark pine grove, I found a gravestone, overgrown with green moss and broken by the hand of time—

with great difficulty I was able to read the following inscription: "Aleksei Liuboslavskii and his spouse are buried here." Old people told me that at one time an old church stood on this spot—probably the same church in which our lovers were wed and where they wanted to live even after their death.

1792

The Island

of

Bornholm

FRIENDS! Beautiful summer has passed; golden autumn has paled; the greenery has faded; trees stand without fruit and without leaves; the misty sky surges like a sullen sea; the wintry down falls on the cold earth—let us bid farewell to Nature until the joyous vernal meeting; let us take shelter from blizzards and snowstorms—let us take shelter in our quiet study! Time should not burden us; we know a remedy for boredom. Friends! The oak and birch are ablaze in our hearth—let the wind rage and pile up our windows with white snow. Let us sit around the crimson fire and tell one another fairy tales, stories, and all sorts of true happenings.

You know that I have wandered in foreign lands, far, far from my fatherland, far from you, dear ones of my heart; I have seen many wonderful things, heard many amazing things; I have told you much, but could not tell you everything that happened to me. Listen—I will tell you a story—I will tell you a true story, not a figment of my imagination.

England was the farthest compass of my journey. There I said to myself: "Your fatherland and friends are waiting for you; it is time to rest in their embraces; it is time to dedicate your pilgrim's staff to the son of Maia †; it is time to hang it on the heaviest branch of that tree beneath which you frolicked in your youth"—I said this and boarded the ship "Britannia" in London to sail to the dear lands of Russia.

Under white sails we moved rapidly along the flowering banks of the majestic Thames. Soon the limitless sea loomed blue before us; soon we heard the noise of its surging—but suddenly the wind shifted and our ship had to stop opposite the small town of Gravesend to await a more propitious time.

Together the captain and I went ashore; with peace of heart I roamed over green meadows adorned by Nature and diligence—sites rare and picturesque; finally, fatigued by the sun's heat, I lay down on the grass, beneath a century-old elm, near the seashore and looked at the watery expanse, at the foamy billows which in countless lines from the obscured distance rushed with a dull roar to the island. This doleful noise and view of the boundless waters began to induce a drowsiness in me, that pleasurable quiescence of the soul in which all ideas and feelings stop and become rigid, like the streams of a spring which are frozen suddenly, and which is

† In ancient times wanderers, upon returning to their fatherland, dedicated their staffs to Mercury.

the most striking and the most poetic image of death; but suddenly the branches shook above my head. . . . I glanced up and saw—a young man, thin, pale, languid—more specter than man. In one hand he held a guitar, with the other he plucked leaflets from the tree and looked at the dark-blue sea with his motionless dark eyes, in which shone the last ray of a flickering life. My gaze could not meet his; his feelings were dead to external objects; he stood two paces from me, but saw nothing, heard nothing. "Unfortunate young man!" thought I. "You have been destroyed by fate. I know neither your name nor your origin; but I do know that you are unhappy."

He sighed, raised his eyes heavenward—lowered them again to the waves of the sea—walked away from the tree, sat upon the grass, began to play a sad prelude upon his guitar while looking continually at the sea, and he began to sing softly the following song (in Danish, which my friend, Doctor N.N.,[1] had taught me in Geneva):

> The laws condemn
> The object of my love;
> But who, O heart! can
> Oppose you?
>
> What law is more sacred
> Than your innate feelings?
> What power is stronger
> Than love and beauty?

1. In his first letter from Basel (*Letters of a Russian Traveler*), Karamzin describes his meeting with Gottfried Becker (1767–1845), who had studied medicine and chemistry in Germany. Becker, the son of the apothecary to the Danish court, was wandering through Europe on foot. Later, in Geneva, Karamzin met him again and they passed most of the autumn and winter of 1789–90 in close company.

I love—I shall love forever;
Curse my passion,
Pitiless souls,
Cruel hearts!

Holy Nature!
Your tender friend and son
Is innocent before you.
You gave me a heart;

Your righteous gifts
Do adorn it—
Nature! You desired
That I love Lila!

Your thunder rumbled over us,
But did not strike us,
When we delighted
In the embrace of love.

O Bornholm, sweet Bornholm!
My soul craves
For thee incessantly;
But I shed tears in vain,

I languish and sigh!
I have been forced,
By a parental oath, to withdraw
Forever from your shores!

Do you still, O Lila!
Live with your anguish?
Or have you ended this evil life
In the roaring waves?

Appear before me, appear,
Dearest shade!
I shall be buried with you
In the roaring waves.

Here an involuntary, inner urge made me want to throw
myself on the stranger and press him to my heart, but at that
very moment my captain took me by the arm and said that a
favorable wind had billowed our sails and that we should not
lose any time.—We sailed. The young man, guitar put aside
and arms folded, watched us—watched the dark-blue sea.

The waves foamed under the helm of our ship, the Gravesend shore was hidden in the distance, the northern provinces
of England grew dark on the other edge of the horizon—finally everything vanished, and the birds, which had hovered
over us a long time, flew back to the shore, as if frightened by
the boundlessness of the sea. The surge of the noisy waters and
the misty sky were the only objects of our eyes, objects majestic and terrible.—My friends! In order to feel intensely all the
audacity of the human spirit, one has to be on the open sea,
where only *a small, thin plank,* as Wieland says, *separates us
from a watery death,* but where the skillful sailor, unfurling
the sails, flies on and in his mind already sees the glitter of
gold with which his daring enterprise will be rewarded in
another part of the world. *"Nil mortalibus arduum est—nothing is impossible for mortals"*—I thought with Horace, losing
my gaze in the infinity of Neptune's kingdom.

But soon a severe attack of seasickness deprived me of
consciousness. For six days my eyes were not opened, my
languid heart, washed by the foam of stormy waves,† barely
beat in my chest. On the seventh day I revived and went on

† Indeed, the foam of the waves often washed over me, as I lay
almost unconscious on the deck.

deck with a pale but happy face. The sun had already moved through the clear, azure vault of heaven toward the west; the sea, lighted by its golden rays, roared; under full sail the ship flew on over the masses of sundered billows, which vainly endeavored to outstrip it. Around us, at various distances, fluttered white, blue, and pink flags, but on the right something like land loomed dark.

"Where are we?" I asked the captain.

"Our voyage has been successful," he said; "we have passed Zund; the shores of Sweden have disappeared from view. On the right you see the Danish island of Bornholm, a dangerous place for ships; shoals and rocks are concealed there on the sea floor. When night falls, we shall drop anchor."

"The island of Bornholm, the island of Bornholm," I repeated in my thoughts, and the image of the young Gravesend stranger revived in my soul. The sad sounds and words of his song echoed in my ear. "They contain the secret of his heart," I thought; "but who is he? What laws condemn the love of the unfortunate? What oath forced him to leave the shores of Bornholm, so sweet to him? Shall I, sometime, find out his story?"

Meanwhile a strong wind carried us straight toward the island. Its threatening crags had already appeared, whence seething streams, roaring and foaming, hurtled into the sea's depth. It seemed inaccessible on all sides, protected on all sides by the majestic hand of Nature; nothing but the terrible appeared on those gray cliffs. With horror, I saw there the image of cold, silent eternity, the image of implacable death and that indescribably creative power before which everything mortal must tremble.

The sun sank in the waves—and we cast anchor. The wind had fallen, and the sea scarcely moved. I looked at the island, which drew me with an inexplicable force to its shores; a vague foreboding spoke to me: "There you can satisfy your curiosity, and Bornholm will remain indelibly in your memory!"—Finally, having discovered that there were fishermen's huts not far from the shore, I decided to ask the captain for a dinghy and go to the island with two or three seamen. He spoke of the danger, the submerged rocks, but, seeing the inflexibility of his passenger, he agreed to satisfy my demand on the condition that I return to the ship early the next morning.

We set off and safely pulled up to the shore of a small, quiet cove. Here we were greeted by fishermen, coarse and primitive people, reared by the cold elements in the noise of the sea's billows and unacquainted with the smile of friendly greeting; on the other hand, they were neither crafty nor evil people. When they heard that we wished to look over the island and spend the night in their huts, they tied up our boat and led us over a crumbling siliceous hill toward their dwellings. In half an hour we came out on an expansive green plain where, as in Alpine valleys, were scattered low-slung little wooden houses, small groves, and masses of stone. Here I left the seamen and went on alone in order to enjoy a little longer the pleasantness of the evening; a boy of some thirteen years was my guide.

The crimson glow had not yet faded in the bright sky; its pink light fell on the white granite and, in the distance, behind a high hill, lighted the spired towers of an ancient castle. The boy was not able to tell me to whom this castle belonged.

"We do not go there," he said. "God only knows what goes on there!"

I doubled my pace and soon drew near a large Gothic building, which was encircled by a deep moat and a high wall. Silence reigned everywhere, in the distance the sea roared, the last ray of the evening light had died out on the copper spires of the towers.

I walked around the castle—the gates were locked, the

bridges drawn. My guide was afraid of something, he himself did not know of what, and implored me to go back to the huts, but could a curious man comply with such a request?

Night came, and suddenly a voice rang out—an echo repeated it, and again all was silent. In fear, the boy grabbed me with both arms and trembled like a criminal at the moment of execution. In a minute a voice rang out again asking: "Who is there?"

"A foreigner," I said, "led to this island by curiosity, and if hospitality is considered a virtue in the walls of your castle, then you will shelter a wanderer during the dark of night."

There was no answer, but in a few minutes the drawbridge began to clank and was lowered from the top of the tower, and the gates opened noisily—a tall man in a long black dress met me, took me by the hand, and led me into the castle. I turned around but the boy who had accompanied me had disappeared.

The gates slammed behind us; the bridge clanked and was raised. We walked across a vast courtyard, overgrown with bushes, nettles, and wormwood, toward a huge house in which a light glowed. A high peristyle in an antique manner led to an iron porch whose steps rang beneath our feet. It was gloomy and deserted everywhere. In the first hall, encircled within by a Gothic colonnade, hung a lamp and it shed a weak, dim light upon a row of gilded pillars which had begun to crumble, worn by time; pieces of the cornice lay in one spot, fragments of the pilasters in another; in still another, entire fallen columns. My guide glanced at me several times with his penetrating eyes, but spoke not a word.

All this made a strange impression on my heart, mixed in part with horror, in part with a secret inexplicable pleasure or, better, with the pleasant expectation of something extraordinary.

We passed through two or three more halls, similar to the

first and lighted by the same kind of lamps. Then a door opened to the right—in a corner of the small room sat a venerable, gray-haired old man, leaning upon a table where two white wax candles burned. He raised his head, glanced at me with a kind of sad tenderness, offered me his feeble hand, and said in a soft, pleasant voice: "Although eternal grief dwells within the walls of this castle, yet the wanderer, who demands hospitality, will always find a peaceful refuge here. Foreigner! I do not know you, but you are a man—in my dying heart love still exists for people—my house, my embraces are open to you." He embraced me, seated me, and, trying to enliven his gloomy visage, he seemed like a clear but cold autumn day, recalling rather a grieving winter than joyous summer. He seemed to want to be kind—to want by a smile to inspire in me trust and pleasant feelings of friendliness, but the marks of spiritual sorrow which furrowed his face could not disappear at once.

"You must, young man," said he, "you must inform me of the events of a world which I have abandoned but not entirely forgotten. Long have I lived in solitude, long have I heard nothing of the fate of people. Tell me, does love reign on the terrestrial sphere? Does incense burn on altars of virtue? Do the people of lands you have seen prosper?" "The light of science," I answered, "extends further and further, but human blood still flows on the earth—the tears of the unfortunate flow—they praise the name of virtue and argue about its essence." The old man sighed and shrugged his shoulders.

Having found out that I was a Russian, he said: "We are descended from the same people as you. The ancient inhabitants of the islands Rügen and Bornholm were Slavs. But you were enlightened by the light of Christianity before us. Magnificent temples, dedicated to one God, had already risen to the clouds in your lands, but we in the darkness of idolatry were offering bloody sacrifices to insensate images. In solemn hymns you had already glorified the great creator of the universe, but we, blinded by error, praised in dissonant songs the idols of mythology." The old man spoke with me about the history of northern peoples, about events of antiquity and modern times; he spoke in such a way that I was amazed at his mind, knowledge, and even his eloquence.

In half an hour he got up and wished me a good night. The servant in the dark dress, having taken a candle from the table, led me through long narrow passages—and we entered a large room, hung with ancient weapons, swords, lances, cuirasses, and spiked helmets. In a corner under a golden canopy stood a high bedstead, adorned with fretwork and antique bas-relief.

I wanted to pose many questions to this man, but he, without waiting for them, bowed and left; the iron door slammed—the sound reverberated terribly within the empty walls—and all became quiet. I lay down on the bed—looked at the ancient weapons, which through the small window were lighted by the faint ray of the moon—thought about my host, about his first words: "Here dwells eternal grief"—dreamed about times past, about those adventures which this ancient castle had witnessed—dreamed like a man who amid coffins and graves gazes at the dust of the dead and revives them in his imagination.—Finally the image of the sad Gravesend stranger rose in my soul, and I fell asleep.

But my sleep was not peaceful. It seemed to me that all the cuirasses hanging on the wall had changed into knights, that these knights approached me with drawn swords, and with angry looks said, "Unfortunate man! How dare you land on our island? Do not seafarers grow pale at the sight of its granite shores? How dare you enter the terrible sanctuary of the castle? Is not its horror known through all the environs? Does not the wanderer retreat from its menacing towers? Daring man! Die for this baleful curiosity!" The swords

began to bang above me, blows rained down on my chest—
but suddenly everything vanished—I awoke and in a minute
again fell asleep. Here a new dream disturbed my spirit. It
seemed to me that a terrible thunder resounded through the
castle, the iron doors banged, windows rattled, the floor shook,
and a horrible winged monster, which I do not know how to
describe, with a roar and a shriek flew toward my bed. The
vision disappeared but I could no longer sleep, felt the need
for some fresh air, approached the window, saw beside it a
small door, opened it, and by a steep staircase—descended into
the garden.

The night was clear, the light of the full moon silvered the
dark greenery of ancient oaks and elms, which formed a dense
long lane. The noise of the ocean waves joined the noise of the
leaves, rustled by the wind. In the distance were whitened
rocky masses, which, like a crenelated wall, encircled the
island of Bornholm; between these and the walls of the castle
could be seen a large forest on one side—an open plain and
small groves on the other.

My heart was still pounding from the terrible visions and
my blood had not ceased its agitated pulsating. I entered the
dark lane, beneath the cover of the rustling oaks, and with a
feeling of deep reverence walked deeper into its darkness. A
thought of Druids stirred in my soul—and it seemed to me
that I was approaching that sanctuary where all the mysteries
and all the horrors of their worship are preserved. At last this
long lane led me to rosemary shrubs, behind which a sandy
hill towered. I wanted to ascend its summit in order to look at
the panorama of the sea and the island in the clear moonlight,
but here an opening into the hill became visible: a man could
with difficulty enter it. An irresistible curiosity drew me into
this cavern, which seemed more the work of human hands
than a product of wild Nature. I entered—I felt a dampness
and coldness but decided to go farther and, having taken some

ten steps forward, discerned several descending steps and a wide iron door; to my astonishment, it was not locked. My hand opened it, seemingly without my will—here behind an iron grating, on which a large lock hung, there burned a lamp, attached to the vault, while in a corner on a straw bed lay a pale young woman in a black dress. She was sleeping; her light-brown hair, entangled with yellow straws, covered her high bosom, which was just barely moving; one hand, white but emaciated, lay on the ground, while the head of the sleeping woman rested on the other. Had an artist wished to portray a languishing, endless, constant grief, strewn with the poppies of Morpheus, then this woman could have served as a beautiful model for his brush.

My friends! Who is not touched by the sight of an unfortunate? But the sight of a young woman, suffering in a dungeon—the sight of the weakest and most beloved of all beings oppressed by fate—could infuse the very stone with feeling. I looked at her with grief and thought to myself: "What barbarian hand has deprived you of the light of day? Is it possible, for some serious crime? But your comely face, but the soft movement of your bosom, but my own heart assure me of your innocence!"

At this very moment she awoke—glanced at the grating, saw me—was dumfounded—raised her head—arose—drew near—lowered her eyes to the ground, as if collecting her thoughts—again fixed her eyes on me, wanted to speak and—did not begin.

"If the sensitivity of a wanderer," I said after some moments of silence, "who has been led to this castle and to this cavern by the hand of fate, can ease your lot, if his sincere compassion merits your trust, demand his help!" She looked at me with motionless eyes, in which astonishment was apparent and a certain curiosity, indecision, and doubt. Finally, after an intense inner turmoil, which seemed to shake her bosom as with an electric shock, she answered me in a firm voice: "Whoever you might be, whatever circumstance brought you here—foreigner, I cannot demand of you anything except commiseration. It is not within your power to change my lot. I kiss the hand which punishes me." "But your heart is innocent?" said I. "It, of course, does not merit such cruel punishment?" "My heart," she answered, "could have erred. God will forgive the weak. I hope that my life will soon end. Leave me, stranger!" Here she approached the grating, looked at me tenderly, and with a low voice repeated: "For God's sake, leave me! . . . If he himself sent you—he whose terrible curse thunders constantly in my ear—tell him that I am suffering, suffering day and night, that my heart has wasted away from grief, that tears no longer ease my anguish. Tell him that I shall endure my imprisonment without murmur, without complaints, that I shall die as his tender, unfortunate. . . ."—She suddenly became silent, became pensive, withdrew from the grating, knelt and covered her face with her hands; in a minute she looked at me, again lowered her eyes to the ground, and said with tender shyness: "You, perhaps, know my story, but if you do not, then do not ask me—for God's sake, do not ask! . . . Foreigner, farewell!" Having said a few words to her that flowed straight from my soul, I wanted to go, but my gaze once again met her gaze—and it seemed to me that she wanted to find out from me something of significance to her heart. I stopped—awaiting her question, but after a deep sigh it died on her pale lips. We parted.

I did not close the iron door on leaving the cavern in order that the fresh, clean air might penetrate the dungeon through the grating and ease the breathing of the unfortunate woman. Dawn crimsoned the sky, the little birds awakened, a little breeze blew the dew from the bushes and from the little flowers which grew about the sandy hill. "My God!" I thought. "My God! how grievous to be excluded from the society of living, free, joyous creatures, who everywhere inhabit the boundless expanse of Nature! In the very north, among tall, mossy crags, horrible to behold, the creation of your hand is beautiful—the creation of your hand delights the spirit and heart. Even here, where frothy waves have struggled with the granite cliffs since the beginning of the world—even here your hand has impressed the living signs of creative love and goodness, even here in the morning hours roses bloom beneath the azure sky, even here tender zephyrs exhale fragrances, even here green carpets spread like soft velvet beneath the foot of man, even here the little birds sing—they sing gaily for the gay, sadly for the sad, and pleasantly for all, even here the sorrowing heart can ease its burdens of grief in the embraces of sensitive nature! But—the poor girl, imprisoned in the dungeon, does not have this consolation: the dew of morning does not moisten her languishing heart, the little breeze does not freshen her consumed bosom; the rays of the sun do not light her beclouded eyes; the soft, balsamic effusions of the moon do not nourish her spirit with gentle visions and pleasant dreams. Creator! Why have you bestowed on people the destructive power to make one another and themselves miserable?" Beneath the branches of a tall oak, on the soft greenery, my strength ebbed and my eyes closed.

My sleep lasted some two hours.

"The door had been opened; the foreigner entered the cavern"—that is what I heard on awakening—I opened my eyes and saw the old man, my host; he sat pensively on a turf bench some five feet from me; beside him stood the servant who had led me into the castle. I walked up to them. The old man looked at me with a certain severity, arose, clasped my hand—and his expression became kinder. Together we entered the dense lane; not a word was spoken. It seemed that at heart he wavered and was undecided, but suddenly he stopped and, fixing his penetrating, fiery gaze on me, asked in a firm voice: "Did you see her?" "I saw her," I answered, "I saw, without knowing who she was and why she suffers in the dungeon." "You will find out," he said, "you will find out, young man, and your heart will be drenched in blood. Then you will ask yourself: why has Heaven poured out the whole cup of its wrath on this weak, gray-haired old man, an old man who loved virtue, who honored its sacred laws?"

We sat beneath the tree and the old man told me a most horrible story—a story which you will not hear now, my friends; it will wait until another time. This time I shall tell you one thing only, that I have found the secret of the Gravesend stranger—a terrible secret!

The sailors awaited me at the gates of the castle. . . . We returned to the ship, set sail, and Bornholm disappeared from sight.

The sea roared. In grieving pensiveness I stood on the deck, grasping the mast with my hand. Sighs crowded my chest—finally I glanced at the sky—and the wind blew my tear into the sea.

1793

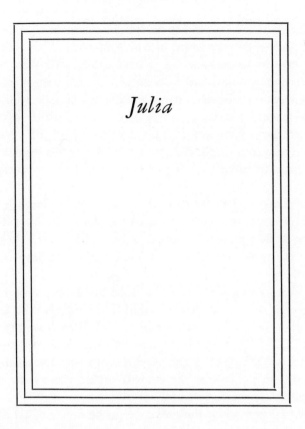

Julia

WOMEN COMPLAIN ABOUT MEN, men about women: who is innocent? who is guilty? who can decide this litigation?—If the decision be mine, then I, without a hearing or an investigation, shall acquit . . . the most lovable—consequently, the women! . . . Without doubt. But the men will be dissatisfied with my decision: they will point to my bias; they will declare that I have been bribed . . . by the sweet glance of some Lydia, by the pleasant smile of some Arethea; they will carry the case to the highest court, and my verdict will remain— alas!—without any effect.

133

This is a brief foreword to the following tale.

Julia was the adornment of our capital; she appeared and the men looked only at her, were occupied only with her, listened only to her. And the women? . . . The women spoke very quietly among themselves and glanced at Julia with an arch smile, attempting to note some failing which would placate their self-esteem just a bit. A vain attempt! Julia shone as the sun; envy sought dark spots in it, did not find them, and with eyes smarting, with despair in its heart, had . . . to clear out!

Is it necessary to say that all the young men adored Julia and considered it an honor to adore her? One sighed, another wept, a third played the role of a languishing melancholic; and, if anyone was pensive, they said: "He is in love with Julia!"

What about Julia? Most of all, she loved—her very own self; with a proud smile she looked to the right, to the left, and thought: "Who is comparable to me? Who is worthy of me?" *She thought this* I beg you to note; but *she did not show it.* Amazed at her beauty and mind, everyone was also amazed, among other things, at the modesty of her glances: an art peculiar only to sweet women.

But in approaching the end of the second decade of her life, Julia gradually began to feel that the incense of vanity is smoke—while quite pleasant, still smoke, which poorly nourishes the soul. However you adore yourself; however you admire your virtues—it is not enough! It is necessary to love something beside the magic letter "I"—and Julia began to examine quite carefully the innumerable host of her suitors. Sometimes her glance favored the young Legkoum [Lightminded], who, as far as beauty was concerned, could vie with Cupid himself; and he occupied himself with nothing but Julia and—the mirror; sometimes, the well-shaped Khrabron [Courageous], a warrior crowned with laurels, who lacked only a Grecian mantle to be a perfect Mars; sometimes, the amusing Pustoslov [Idle-word], who, despite the gravity of his judicial rank, twirled on one leg as Vestris, composed ten French puns every day, and knew the *lexicon of anecdotes* by heart. No one interested her for long—after a moment, Legkoum seemed a rash, vain scamp; Khrabron, an obvious dragoon, and nothing more; the amusing Pustoslov, a boring monkey. Finally, her eyes were fixed on amiable Aris, who really was amiable; the scales inclined in his favor and the heart this time agreed with the mind.

Who was Aris? A young man who had been educated in foreign lands not by a hired tutor but by his wise and tender father. Useful and pleasant knowledge adorned his soul; virtuous principles, his heart. Since he was not handsome, he pleased with his comeliness and gentle, amiable glances, which were enlivened by the fire of inner feeling. He blushed as an innocent maid at any immodest word uttered in his presence; he spoke little but always soundly and pleasantly; he did not try to sparkle through his intelligence or through his knowledge and listened to everyone—at least with patience. Is the value of such people appreciated in society? Rarely. There tinsel is sometimes preferred to the real thing; modesty, the friend of virtues, remains in the shadows while boldness earns the garland and the applause.

Aris loved Julia—how could one not love that which is beautiful and amiable?—but the countless multitude of her adorers terrified him. He looked on her from afar, he did not sigh, he did not place his hands on his heart with a languid mien; in a word, he did not try to appear a picture-book lover: but Julia knew that he loved her passionately. Wonder, if you wish, at the perspicacity of beautiful women! They will not observe the sun at noon on a clear day sooner than the effects of their charms in the eyes of a tender man, however he tries to hide his feelings. Julia distinguished Aris from her other suitors, encouraged his shyness with a pleasant look, a pleasant smile; she began to speak to him, flatter him, show respect for his virtues, attention to his words, desire to see him more often. "Tomorrow you will be at the concert, in the garden; tomorrow you will dine, sup with us; yesterday was boring: you did not want to visit us!" Aris was not one of those people who accept the slightest flattery of women as a proof of love and consider themselves happy Adonises even when the women are not even thinking of them; however, despite his modesty, he allowed himself to hope; and hope is to passion as the soft April rain to young vegetation, as the wind to embers. He was ready to fall to his knees and say to Julia, "Be mine forever." . . . which is what Julia expected, what she wanted, and of course she would not answer "No!" when suddenly a new phenomenon appeared on the horizon of society and attracted general attention: young Prince N*, a favorite of Nature and fortune, which lavished all their glittering gifts on him; aristocratic, rich, and handsome. In all circles of society they spoke of the young Prince; everyone praised him, but most of all the women, especially those at whom he looked more tenderly—to whom he spoke five or six pleasant words. They could not cease admiring his intelligence—even when he spoke about the weather. Is it any wonder—an excited imagination is a microscope which magnifies everything a thousand, a million times—and people of such determination can seek out wit where it is not; sometimes with equal determination they do not want to perceive it where it is.

Meanwhile, the rumor spread through the town that the Prince was indifferent to feminine charms; that Amour's arrows could not find his heart; that it, by a secret, elastic power, could contract and remain unharmed; that Venus' poor son, wishing to wound him, had emptied his quiver and all in vain. What a challenge to the self-esteem of women, what glory to the conqueror! And it seemed to each of them that Cupid, grieving, wailing, drew near, took her by the hand and with a touching glance said: "Revenge me, revenge me, or I shall die of grief!" "Cupid die! My God! How terrible! Why live in this world without the charming babe? It is necessary to intercede for him; it is necessary to help him, it is necessary to take revenge, and—whatever the cost—to move, conquer, capture the new Alcides"—and all the goldsmiths in our capital were busy with one task: to hammer out chains at the order of the beauties.† Be fearful, giddy Prince! But the Prince smiled, strutted about like a proud swan, and—at one public gathering—met Julia. All the beauties were after him, all the young men, after her—what a meeting! They looked at one another: what a glance! Julia eclipsed the women, Prince N*, the men. "He has to love her!" thought the former. "She has to love him!" thought the latter. The one and the other, downcast, bade farewell to hope and went off in different directions.—Only Aris remained beside Julia. He began to speak: she answered him dryly, tersely—she seemed to be distracted.

Aris visited Julia the next day; but a headache did not allow her to leave her room. He glimpsed her at a ball on the third day: The Prince sat by her side—the Prince danced with her —the Prince engaged her in a pleasant conversation. Aris was greeted politely—*politely*—nothing more. He was asked, "How are you?" No one waited for his answer. Aris approached from the other side: he was not observed—and how could he be? He did not approach from the Prince's side.— Poor Aris! Make your surmises. You could have been happy; but the moment has passed! What is to be done? Withdraw. —He did just that, it is not necessary to say with what emotion.—Let us leave him.—Let us weep for a while in seclusion and, if it is possible, forget the sweet giddy creature.

Meanwhile Julia was delighted with the Prince. Silent, he

† This is why golden chains became fashionable; some time before this, they jingled and glittered on all our young women.

seemed an Antinoüs †; when he spoke, a Cicero; when he spoke these words: *Julia, I adore you!*, a demigod. He did not deceive her and really was captivated by her beauty, so much so that he did not want to attend a single concert unless Julia sang there; nor a single ball unless Julia danced there; nor a single promenade unless Julia promenaded there. Previously, he loved to play cards: for Julia, he gave this up. He loved to drive his English horses some three hours a day; for Julia, he forgot them. He loved to sleep until two in the afternoon; for Julia, he changed this habit and often awoke at noon that he might on the wings of Zephyrus—or, at least, in a magnificent English carriage—fly to Julia.—Such a love is no joke. You will say that in the age of chivalry they loved differently—sirs! every century has its own customs: we are living in the eighteenth! Our beauties are indulgent and compassionate; and not one of them, sitting in a box seat, would throw their glove on the mane of an infuriated lion and send her chevalier after it †† because the chevalier—would not go after it!

Julia thought that the Prince could not live without her: only it seemed strange to her that he, speaking constantly of his heart, never mentioned his hand. Many of her girl friends very quietly congratulated her on such an enviable fiancé; but the fiancé was silent.—Finally, she made him realize her astonishment: The tender Prince was insulted. "Julia doubts the strength of her charms!" he said fervently. "Julia wants to replace the fiery Amour with the cold Hymen! the sweet smile of the former for the eternal sullenness of the latter! a garland

† A famous dandy to whom the Emperor Hadrian dedicated a temple.

†† This happened in France, in the reign of King Francis I, at that time when wild animal fights were a favorite amusement of the court. One young lady, seated in the amphitheater, intentionally dropped her glove on that spot where lions were fighting and said to her chevalier, De Lorge: *"Pick it up—or you do not love me."*

of roses for a chain of iron. Oh, Julia! love does not endure restraints; one word, and all bliss disappears! Could Petrarch love his Laura so ardently in the bonds of matrimony? Ah no! his imagination would not have produced one of those tender sonnets which I delight in. So must one love, and Julia is worthy of such a love!" Meanwhile, Julia had grown pale. The Prince saw that she did not like his philosophy; it was necessary to alter his language to placate the beauty.—"At least," he said, "let us prolong, as much as possible, the time of our love: it really will never, never return, charming Julia!" —Here he sighed. Julia could not agree with him; she demanded a promise. The Prince gave it—and as a reward he wanted her to allow him certain liberties. Ever day he assumed a new privilege . . . two fervid hearts beat so strongly, so closely each to each. . . . But modesty is a necessary virtue even for a storyteller. Furthermore—I do not know why—my own heart beats so strongly when I imagine similar circumstances. . . . Perhaps some dim memories . . . Let us leave this—

Let us leave all the details and say, simply, that there were moments when only the goddess of innocence could save Julia's innocence. She realized the danger, and the Prince was forced to name the day for the triumphal engagement. In anticipation of this day, he exhausted all possible wiles to conquer her resolve—but in vain! At the very moment when she in all human probability would have forgotten herself, she sent him away—at least a step or two, so that he lost all hope of being a happy rogue without the name of consort.

One morning when Julia had opened her eyes and imagined immediately her beloved Prince, a note with the following contents was delivered to her:

You are lovable; but what is more lovable than liberty? It grieves me to part with you; but the thought of eternal duty is still more grievous. The heart knows no laws and ceases loving when it wishes: Just what will matrimony be? an unendurable burden. You did not want to love in my fashion, to love only for the pleasure of love—to love while you are in love; and so—farewell! Call me perfidious, if you wish; but it has long been said in the world that the oath of lovers is written in sand and that the slightest little breeze covers it. On the other hand, with such sweet qualities, with such charms, it will not be difficult for you to find a worthy spouse, perhaps, devoted, constant! Phoenixes are born—but I, in this sense, am not a Phoenix; and, therefore, I leave you in peace. I am no longer in Moscow. Farewell!

PRINCE N*

Julie began to tremble and, following the practice of the new Didos, fell into a swoon. After several minutes she gained consciousness only to pass out again. Finally, having collected her strength, she found a certain relief in damning men. "They are all monsters, scoundrels, perfidious; a tigress has suckled them with her milk; beneath their tongue is the serpent's poison and in their heart a viper hisses. Their tears are crocodile's tears; believe them and destruction is inescapable!"—In such tender colors did the desperate Julia paint our portrait. It is pardonable; but is it fair? Are the hearts of men cast in one mold? Can all be responsible for one? . . . But an impassioned individual is a bad logician: *one* seems to him *all,* and *all, one.*

Not later than the following day the breakup of our lovers was known in the town. "Prince N* has left Julia!" said the men, shrugging their shoulders. "Prince N * has left Julia!" said the women with treacherous smiles—and each of them thought, "He would not have left me!"—How could she appear in society? Julia had come to detest it and for a time did not leave her room.

Some two weeks after this event, Aris visited her. She thought a while . . . and ordered him to be admitted.—Poor

Aris! he had to suffer together with all men the arrows of
Julia's eloquence and to listen with the air of a repentant criminal when inconstancy and perfidy were rebuked! Another
man in his position would have looked at Julia with such eyes
that she of course would have become embarrassed and silent;
but the good Aris loved her, could not overcome his passion,
and had not visited the distressed beauty to take vengeance.

Julia was pleased by his visit; she wished to see him a
second, a third time—and after a while her heart stopped
seething in anger against men. Aris' tenderness, meekness,
spiritual virtues, which she had not felt so deeply and keenly
in the tumult of society, touched her soul in the sincere
conversations of her quiet room. "Why," said Julia through
tears, "why are other men not like you! The most tender
inclinations of our hearts would not, then, be a source of
yearning and grief." Aris took advantage of this moment, and
Julia could not refuse his hand, on the condition that they
leave forever this *"treacherous world"*—as she said, trying to
efface the last traces of the frivolous Prince N* from her
thoughts.—"A treacherous world, which is not worthy to
witness our happiness, dear Aris! Let us scorn its vanity—I
cannot endure it—and withdraw to the country!"—"All my
days," he answered through joyous tears, "will be devoted to
your pleasure, incomparable Julia! I would be glad to live
with you at the end of the earth; never, never shall I insult
you, neither by a glance, nor by a reproach, nor by a com-
plaint.—Your will is my command; you make me happy; to
divine your wishes, to fulfill them, to depend on you completely is the sacred obligation of my gratitude!"—Aris will
not deceive Julia; but Julia—we shall see!

Their first six or seven weeks in the country passed as six or
seven merry days. The virtuous consort was delighted every
hour, every minute with his charming wife. Julia was responsive to his tenderness—and their hearts joined in quiet rap-

tures. It seemed that Nature herself took part in their joys: she bloomed there in all the expanse of her gardens. The sweet smell of jasmine and lilies of the valley was everywhere; nightingales and robins sang everywhere; the incense of love burned everywhere, and everything pleasurably nourished the love of our conjugal pair.

"My God! (said Julia) how can people live in town! How can they move from the country! There, tumult and restlessness; here, pure, innocent pleasure. There, eternal constraint; here, peace and freedom. Ah, my friend! . . . (with a touching glance she took Aris' hand and pressed it to her breast). . . . Ah, my friend! only in rural quiet alone, in the embrace of Nature alone, can the sensitive soul enjoy all the amplitude of love and tenderness!"

At the end of the summer Julia still praised rural life, but not with the same eloquence, not with the same fervor. But— gloomy autumn follows beautiful summer. Then the flowers in the field and garden faded; the greenery grew pale; the leaves flew from the trees; the little birds. . . . God knows where they had gone—and everything became so sad, so doleful, that Julia lost all desire to praise country solitude. Aris had observed that in looking out of the window she often covered her little crimson mouth with a white handkerchief and that the white handkerchief, as though from the wafting of Zephyrus, rose and fell—that is, simply, Julia yawned! Aris sighed—took a volume of *La Nouvelle Héloïse,* opened it and read several pages . . . on the bliss of a mutual love. Julia stopped yawning, listened, and finally said: "It is beautiful! only, do you know, my friend? It seems to me that Rousseau wrote more from his imagination than from his heart. It would be good if things were so; but are they really like that? The pleasure of a happy love is the prime pleasure in life; but can it always be uniformly vivacious, always satisfy the soul? can it replace all other pleasures? can it people the wilderness for us? Ah, the human heart is insatiable; it constantly desires something new, new impressions, which like the morning dew refresh its inner feelings and give them new strength. For example, I think that the warmest love can grow cold in complete solitude; it needs to compare in order to recognize the value of its object all the more."—Aris sighed and said: "I don't think so; but . . . tomorrow we shall return to town!"

Julia once again appeared in society and with a new luster to her beauty, with wealth, with splendor: this was enough— society received her with applause, and roses were strewn on Julia from all sides. Merriment followed merriment, pleasure followed pleasure—just as before—with this difference, that a married woman has a still greater latitude to enjoy all the pleasantries of social life.

Our heroine wanted an open house, so at least four times a week thirty or forty people supped at her table. Aris was silent; he did everything to please her. Julia recognized this tenderness and, when alone with him, rewarded him with her delightful caresses. "Isn't it true, my friend"—she said with a charming smile—"that the amusements of town and the variety of objects revitalize our love even more? My heart, exhausted by the social tumult, enjoys repose in this embrace." —Aris sighed—so quietly that Julia did not hear.

But once, toward evening, Aris changed countenance—he saw Prince N* among the guests who had come to visit Julia! His heart began to pound; however, after several minutes this involuntary agitation was controlled. The mind told the heart: *Be silent!* and Aris walked up to the Prince with a polite greeting. Only during the entire evening he was afraid to look too long at Julia, lest she misinterpret his glances and discover some sort of suspicion, concern, displeasure in them.

After supper, when everyone had gone, Julia sat down on the sofa, took Aris by the hand, and said with a smile: "You saw, my friend, how politely I treated Prince N*. Not to receive him, to exclude him from my home, would have been foolish on my part. Let this frivolous Narcissus see that he means nothing to me; that my past error has not left a mark on my soul; that I do not have any reason to fear my heart and that he cannot embarrass me."—Aris, Aris kissed her hand and rendered justice to the wisdom of his spouse.

In two days there was another supper, and the Prince again appeared with the other guests; he was merry, amusing; he spoke more with the hostess than with anyone else; he did not consider the host; he glanced at him almost with scorn and conducted himself as a man of fashion should. To put it briefly, he did not miss a chance to visit Julia. "How merry it is in her home!" said the men and women. "The hostess is as amiable as an angel," said the former. "The sweet Prince N* spreads pleasure about him," said the latter. Meanwhile, talk began. Some looked at Aris with a sneer; others shrugged their shoulders. "What is there to be amazed at?" they whispered to one another. "It's an old friendship! Now there is even less danger. The husband is quiet, unassuming—that's the end of the matter!"

Aris did not change in regard to Julia; but he soon saw a change in her. Sometimes she became pensive, grew pale, wanted to be alone; after an hour a most tender glow suffused her face: she threw herself into her consort's embrace, kissed him fervently, wanted to say something and spoke not a word. The unassuming Aris was also silent; sometimes tears rolled from his eyes—but who witnessed them? the quiet solitude; a dense tree-lined lane of his garden, which, after Julia, became dearest of all to him. It seemed to Aris that its cold shadows feelingly touched his heart and were warmed by his body heat.

One day, toward evening, he came home and hurried to his beloved lane; he entered—and saw Prince N*, seated on the raised turf beside Julia, who, her head on his shoulder, looked at the earth. He was kissing her hand and saying: "You love

144

me and I must die in your embrace! Julia! Why do you have these prejudices? Follow the urging of your heart; follow. . . ." But Julia heard a rustling, looked up—and began to tremble. . . . Imagine yourself in poor Aris' place! . . . What was to be done? Slay both with one dagger; appease the thirst for a just revenge with blood; and then, . . . kill himself as well. . . . No! Aris struggled with himself—not more than a minute; a terrible minute—but he quelled his seething heart and disappeared!—A man who saw him leaving the lane told me that he was pale as a ghost; that his legs shook perceptibly; that a dumb moan, seemingly wrenched from him, burst from his heart; that he, looking at the heavens and sighing several times, left suddenly at a rapid pace.

That very evening the following letter was delivered to Julia:

I have not broken my word; I have offended you neither with complaints nor reproaches; I trusted the strength of my tenderness and love; I was deceived and must endure!—After what I saw and heard . . . we cannot live together. I do not want to burden you with my presence. The rights of matrimony are insufferable when love does not sanctify them. Julia—farewell! . . . You are free! Forget that you had a consort; for a long time —perhaps never again, will you hear of him! An ocean will separate us. I shall have neither a fatherland nor friends; I shall have one feeling, for grief and melancholy!—In the accompanying parcel you will find directions by which you can dispose of my estate; you will also find a portrait—of my former spouse. . . . No, I shall take it with me; I shall speak with it as with the shade of a dead friend; as with the sole and last sweet object of a dying heart!

It is necessary to know that Julia, having glimpsed Aris in the lane, sat silently for several minutes; then she rushed after him, called him two times by name . . . her voice broke, her legs gave way—she had to lean on the shoulder of the Prince and was scarcely able to reach the house. Not seeing Aris there, she collapsed on the sofa, covered her face with her hands, and spoke not a word. Vainly, the obliging Prince approached her, he tried vainly to calm her—she was silent.

Julia grasped Aris' letter with a trembling hand—read it through—and tears in three streams rolled from her eyes. The Prince wanted to take the letter. . . . "Stop!" she said in a firm voice: "You cannot read it; it was written by a virtuous man! The fog has lifted—and I scorn myself! . . . O women! you complain of the treachery of men: your frivolity, your inconstancy, serve to justify them. You do not appreciate the value of a tender, virtuous heart; you want to please the whole world, you chase after glittering victories and are the sacrifice of your own vanity †—Sir! you see me for the last time. Deceive other women, mock the weak; only I implore you to forget me, to leave me forever. I blame no one, only my own rashness. There will be no lack of pleasures for you in society; but I loathe you and all such as you. I swear to myself that from this day on bold vice shall not dare to look me straight in the eyes. You are amazed at the sudden change; believe it or not: it is all the same to me."—She spoke and disappeared like lightning.

The Prince stood like a motionless statue; finally, he pulled himself together, began to laugh—sincerely or hypocritically, we shall not say—entered his carriage and drove to a play.

Julia—having ascertained that Aris had left Moscow for parts unknown and accompanied only by his valet—quickly forsook the town and withdrew to the country. "Here my days will pass in quiet solitude," she said with a sigh: "My rural cottage! I could have been happy within your quiet walls but

---

† "Is such a declaration appropriate?" a critic will say, "can a woman in *such* a position preach virtue?" "She *can*," I answer, "she can, she can!" and the proof . . . I will show later.

knew not how to be; I left you with a most worthy, a tender, husband. I return alone, a poor widow, but with a heart that loves virtue. It will be my consolation, my comrade, my friend; I shall view, I shall kiss its images in the features of the unforgettable Aris!"—At this moment her tears dropped on his portrait which she held in her hands.

Justice must be rendered to you, dear women: when you decide on something, not in a frivolous moment, not with words but with your soul, and with the deep feeling of sincerity, your tenacity is always astonishing—and the most glorious Heroes of constancy, whom History extols to the skies, must share their laurels with you.

Julia—who had been within a hairsbreadth of becoming a new Aspasia, a new Laïs—Julia became an angel of purity. All vain desires died in her heart; she devoted her life to the memory of her dear spouse; she imagined him standing before her; she poured out her feelings to him; she said: "You have left me; you had the right to leave me; I do not dare to wish your return—I wish only the serenity of your dear soul; I wish you to forget your wife if her image torments your heart. Be happy, wherever you are! Your sweet shade is with me; the remembrance of your love is with me; I shall not die of grief! I want to live that you might have a tender friend in this world. Perhaps, by some secret bond, your heart, despite the separation, the distance which separates us, will be warmed, will be vivified by my love; perhaps in a deep quiet sleep, the wafting of Zephyrus will tell you: *Aris is not alone in the world*—you will open your sweet eyes and in the distance, in the mist, you will see your grieving Julia, who follows you with her spirit, with her heart; perhaps. . . . Ah! Despite myself I wish . . . No, no! I want to adore him without any hope!"

A quiet despondence, more pleasant than torturous, reigned in her soul. Virtuous feelings are incompatible with yearning:

the bitterest tears of repentance have something sweet in them. The dawn of virtue is also beautiful: and what else is repentance?

Julia soon discovered that she was pregnant: a new powerful feeling, which shook her soul! . . . a joyful or a sad feeling? Julia herself was not able to sort out her thoughts for some time.—"I shall be a mother? . . . But who will take the infant in his arms with a tender smile? Who will shed tears of love and joy over him? To whom shall I say: *here is our son! here is our daughter!* Unhappy infant! You will be born an orphan, and the image of grief will be the first object of your opening eyes! . . . But . . . as it pleases Providence! My new duty is to live and endure without murmur!—Be born, sweet infant! My heart will be a father and mother to you. I shall be consoled because of you and by you; I shall not offend your tender soul with my grievous sighs or my gloomy looks! Only love awaits you in my embrace and the hour of your birth will renew my life!"

Julia wished to prepare herself for the sacred calling of motherhood. *Émile*—the sole book of this type—never left her hands.—"I did not know how to be a virtuous spouse (she said with a sigh), at least I shall be a good mother, I shall make amends for the negligence of *one* obligation by the faithful fulfillment of the *other!*"

She counted the days and minutes: in advance she gave herself completely to the sweet infant, still unborn; in advance she kissed him in her imagination, called him all sorts of tender names—and his every movement was a movement of joy to her.

He was born—a son—a most beautiful baby, uniting the features of his father and mother. Julia did not feel any pain, did not feel any weakness; she was busy with him, only with him, she breathed him; she wept—she smiled to make him smile—and her heart, tasting the sweet feelings of motherhood, found within itself a new source of joy, pure, holy, indescribable joy. Her eyes never tired of looking at the infant; her tongue never tired, calling him *beloved, sweet son* a thousand times! She warmed his young soul with the fire of her love; she carefully observed his initial reactions, from the first tear to his grin, and through her tender glances she poured her very own sensitivity into him.—Is it necessary to say that she herself nursed her son?

It seemed to Julia that all things about her had changed and had become more endearing. Previously, she almost never had left her room; the open sky, the vastness, the immense plains nourished the sad idea of loneliness within her soul. *What am I in the immeasurable range of creation?* she asked herself, and fell into deep reverie. The noise of the river and woods increased her melancholy; the merriment of the passing little birds was alien to her heart. Now Julia hurried to show her small darling all Nature. It seemed to her that the sun shone more brightly on him; that every tree bent to embrace him; that the brooklet caressed him with its purling; that the little birds and butterflies fluttered and sported for his amusement. *I am a mother,* she thought, and walked through the meadow at a brisker pace.

The pleasures which Julia had at one time sought in society now seemed to her an insignificant, deceptive phantom in comparison with the substantial, nourishing delight of motherhood. Ah! she would have been completely happy had not the thought of a grief-laden Aris disturbed her heart. "I shed tears of joy," she said to herself—"I revel in these delights when he in grief-laden solitude wanders through the world, reproaching himself for his love of an unworthy spouse! What angel will inform him of the change in my heart?" Julia could have . . . so, in the presence of Heaven itself, I venture to say that Julia could have now made amends to him for her guilt! . . . "But he does not know; he imagines me in the embrace—of vice; he imagines me dead to all feelings of virtue! . . . Let him return if only for a moment; if only to see our son! Let him—saying: 'You are not worthy to enjoy him'—take him from me! I would be glad to be deprived of all consolations, to console my injured husband. . . . I would be glad to be unhappy for his well-being! And he will be happy; with this angel of beauty and innocence he will forget all sorrows!"

Meanwhile, little Erast † bloomed like a rose; he was already able to run through the meadow; he was able to say to Julia: *I love you, mommie!* he was able to caress her warmly, and with his tender little hands to brush away the pleasant tears which often rolled from her eyes.

Once, in the spring—a time which always reminded Julia of the first spring of her marriage—she went for a walk with her little Erast, sat down on a flowering hillock near the road, and—while the infant frolicked and gamboled about her— took from her bosom Aris' portrait and studied it with tender emotion.—"Is he like this now?" thought Julia. "Ah no! his features have changed of course. When the artist drew them, he was seated opposite me, he looked at me with love, he was merry and happy! And now . . . now.". . . Julia's glance grew dark. She became pensive and a light sleep closed her eyes for a moment.

A disturbed soul also sees disturbing dreams: †† Julia in her sleep saw an immense ocean, which roared and frothed beneath dark storm clouds; sinuous lightning flashed in the darkness, terrible thunder resounded, and horror was everywhere borne on the wings of the storm. Suddenly a vessel appears, a plaything, a sacrifice to the enraged waves—it disappears in the abyss of the seething waters, and reappears to

† Her son's name.

†† *A terrible dream occurs before a happy event,* says a Spanish proverb; I have used it as the ending of my tale.

be lost forever in the depths. . . . Ill-starred seafarers! . . . Julia, seated on a rocky crag, sees the wreck and suffers in her sensitive heart. A strong billow surges toward the shore, casts a man on the sand, and withdraws. Julia hurries to the unfortunate—wants to revive him, and recognizes Aris . . . cold, dead. She trembles, awakens . . . and sees Aris in reality: he is in her embrace, and forever.

I realize the weakness of my pen and, therefore, shall not say another word of this rare event; not a word of the first exclamations which burst directly from the depths of the heart; not a word of the eloquent silence of the first minutes; not a word of the tears of joy and bliss! . . . To depict the picture more touchingly, the reader should imagine that still small Erast, whom Julia had taken in her arms and given to Aris. The infant, taught by Nature, caressed his father and looked at Julia with a smile.†

They have lived in the country for three years now; they live as the most tender lovers, and society does not exist for them. Aris has not changed; he was always an active philosopher. But through her conduct Julia has proved that the frivolity of a young woman can sometimes be a veil or a curtain for the greatest virtues.

Aris' tenderness extends so far that he does not allow Julia to describe her previously giddy character in dark terms.— "You were born to be virtuous," said Aris; "the immodest desire to please, the fruit of an injudicious upbringing and bad examples, produced your momentary aberrations. You had to experience only once the value of a real love, the value of virtue, to reform and to hate vice. You are astonished, my

† "Where had Aris come from?" the curious will ask. He had wandered for several years in foreign lands. A faithful friend, whom he had left in Moscow, kept him informed of Julia. Finally, convinced of her virtue, he flew to his adored wife, to tell her: "I never ceased adoring you!"

friend, at why I was silent and did not want to speak to you of the consequences of your giddiness: I was convinced that reproaches would harden your heart rather than touch its sensitivity. A tender forbearance on the husband's part is the most effective remedy in such a case. Upbraidings, rebukes, would make you think that I was jealous; you would have considered yourself offended—and our hearts might have been alienated from each other forever. The outcome has proved the justice of my system. A separation seemed to me the last resort to be used in your reformation. I left you to the tribunal of your own heart—I confess, not coldly, not without torturous grief—but a ray of hope nourished and did not deceive me! You are mine, completely and forever!"

Sometimes Julia took up arms against women: Aris was their defender. "Believe me, my friend (he said), believe me, depraved women are created by depraved men; the former are evil because the latter do not deserve better."

Aris and Julia were able to disagree on different things; but they agreed on this, that the pleasures of a happily married couple and of parenthood are the best of all earthly pleasures.

1794/6

Articles

On Shakespeare

and His Tragedy,

Julius Caesar

I CONSIDER IT ALMOST A NECESSITY to write a foreword on the publication of this Shakespearean creation.[1] Until now, not a single work of this famous author has been translated into our language; as a consequence, not one of my countrymen, unless he has read Shakespeare in other languages, can have an adequate understanding of him. In general it can be said that we are very poorly acquainted with English literature. I consider it inappropriate to speak of the reason for this here. I

1. The title of this article has been supplied.

shall be satisfied if the attention of my readers is not distracted by the fact that I shall speak only of Shakespeare and his creations.

This author lived in England during the period of Queen Elizabeth and was one of those great spirits, glorifying the ages. His works are dramatic works. Time, this mighty destroyer of everything under the sun, has not yet been able to eclipse the beauty and grandeur of Shakespeare's creations. Almost all England joins in the praise bestowed on this man. Let anyone ask a well-read Englishman: "What do you think of Shakespeare?"—Without any doubt, he will answer: "Shakespeare is great! Shakespeare is inimitable!" All the best English writers who came after Shakespeare have carefully examined the beauties of his productions. Milton, Young, Thomson, and other celebrated creators have used many of his thoughts, variously adorning them. Few writers have probed human nature so deeply as has Shakespeare; few have known so well all the most secret springs of man, his innermost intentions, the differentiation of each passion, each personality, and each way of life, as has this wonderful artist. All his splendid pictures imitate nature directly; all hues of these pictures awe the attentive observer. Every class of man, every age, every passion, every character, speaks its very own language. For each idea he finds an image, for each sensation—an expression, for each movement of the soul—the very best turn of speech. His painting is powerful and his colors are resplendent when he wants to show the radiance of virtue; his brush is extremely cajoling when he depicts the gentle animation of the most tender passions; but this very same brush is titanic when he describes the cruel agitation of the soul.

But this great man also, like others, is not free of the bitter censure of certain poor critics. The famous sophist, Voltaire, attempted to prove that Shakespeare was a very mediocre author full of many and great defects. He said:

On Julius Caesar

Shakespeare wrote without rules; his creations are both tragedies and comedies in one, or tragic-comic-lyric-pastoral farces without plan, without scenic tie, without the unities; an unpleasant mixture of the high and low, of the touching and ridiculous, of true and false witticism, of the amusing and the senseless; they are full of thoughts which are worthy of a wise man and, as well, of nonsense which is only worthy of a fool; they are full of pictures which would bring honor to Homer himself and caricatures which would shame Scarron himself.[2]

2. Karamzin's harsh reference to the "famous sophist," Voltaire, reflects the European literary events of the seventies and eighties and is more a declaration of a literary faith than a personal attack; it is Karamzin's opening volley in the battle with Classicism. Voltaire prided himself on being responsible for the European discovery of Shakespeare and for establishing what he considered the "correct approach" to the English dramatist. In several works which grew out of his sojourn in England (1726–29), Voltaire manifested that paradoxical attitude of dismay and delight which runs through his criticism of Shakespeare. He judged the dramatist by those same classical principles of good taste, decorum, and delicacy of language in which he, Voltaire, had been trained; consequently, he criticizes Shakespeare's violation of the classical rules, his indecent language, his indiscriminate mixture of comedy, farce, and tragedy, in general, his "barbarism," while admitting at the same time the bard's genius, originality, and greatness, which, since it is impossible to imitate, "has been the ruin of the English stage" (*Lettres Philosophiques*). Through his references, translations, adaptations, and imitations of the next several decades, Voltaire made Shakespeare's name, if not his art, familiar in Europe and, unfortunately, established a definite bias against him. However, during this time new aesthetic principles came into play, and with the growth of pre-Romanticism in England and Europe, originality, native genius, and the direct imitation of nature rather than of the ancients were now extolled. Shakespeare was admired for the very traits which Voltaire had criticized in him. This shift of aesthetic standards—with its explicit rejection of Classicism—grated upon the sage of Ferney. In righteous wrath Voltaire rose to defend the principles by which he wrote, if not by which he lived. In the early sixties there appeared his *Appel à toutes*

I consider it superfluous now to refute in detail these opinions, whose purpose is to diminish Shakespeare's glory. I shall only say that all those who have tried to demean his accomplishments could not but reluctantly affirm that there is much in him that is excellent. Man is vain; he is afraid to praise other people in order not to demean, in his opinion, himself by such action. Voltaire is indebted to Shakespeare for some of the finest moments of his own tragedies; but, despite this, he compares him with a fool and ranks him below Scarron. From this, one could have drawn a conclusion which would be very insulting to Voltaire's memory; but I refrain from this, remembering that this man is no longer with us.

That Shakespeare did not adhere to the rules of the theater is true. The real reason for this, I think, was his ardent imagination, which would not be bound by any prescriptions. His spirit soared as an eagle and was not able to measure its soaring as the sparrows measure their flights. He did not want to observe the so-called "unities" which our present dramatic

---

les nations de l'Europe, which as the title implies is an appeal to the tribunal of the European intellectuals to judge between the English stage and the French, between Shakespeare and Corneille, between barbarism and beauty. In the middle seventies Pierre le Tourneur's famous translation of Shakespeare began to appear, the prefatory material of which contained not a word of praise for the successor of Corneille, the discoverer of Shakespeare, that is, for Voltaire himself. Violently angry, the old classicist prepared a letter in which he repeated harshly and indecently all his old jeremiads against Shakespeare, and this letter in a somewhat expurgated form was read by D'Alembert before a public meeting of the French Academy on August 25, 1776. The enthusiasm of the audience, most of whom had not read Shakespeare, indicated that Voltaire had won the battle. However, he eventually lost the war, for the interest in Shakespeare, bulwarked by the rise of pre-Romanticism, continued to grow and to occupy the energy of the young, in Germany, France, and, as Karamzin's own words show, even in that outpost of culture, Russia.

authors so meticulously maintain; he did not want to impose stringent limits to his imagination: He looked only at nature, without worrying at all about anything else. He realized that mortal thought could migrate in an instant from the west to the east, from the ends of the Mogul empire to the borders of England. His genius, like the genius of nature, encompassed in its glance both the sun and the atoms. With equal art he depicted both the hero and the fool, the wise and the unwise, Brutus and the cobbler. His dramas, like the immeasurable theater of nature, are full of variety; taken together, they form a complete whole, which needs no correction from contemporary writers of the theater.

The tragedy which I have translated is one of his best creations. Some are critical of the fact that Shakespeare, having entitled this tragedy *Julius Caesar,* still continues it for two acts after his death; but this criticism will be found to be false if everything is carefully considered. Caesar is murdered in the beginning of the third act but his spirit still lives on; it inspires Octavius and Antony, pursues Caesar's murderers, and eventually destroys them all. The murder of Caesar is the substance of the tragedy; all the acts are based on this murder.

The characters depicted in this tragedy deserve the attention of the readers. Brutus' character is the very best. The French translators of Shakespeare's tragedies speak of him thus:

> Brutus is the rarest, most important, and most entertaining moral character. Antony said of Brutus: "This was a man!" But Shakespeare, who depicted him, could say: "This was a character!" because he really is the most beautiful of all the characters ever depicted in dramatic works.[3]

3. Karamzin used Pierre le Tourneur's French translation of Shakespeare (*Shakespeare.* Traduit de l'Anglois, dédié au Roi [Paris, 1776–83] for his translation of *Julius Caesar* (Vol. II, 1776). Karamzin adapted many of Le Tourneur's ideas as set down in the "Epitre au Roi," "Vie de Shakespeare," "Discours," and the Preface

As far as my translation is concerned, I have tried most of all to translate it faithfully, trying as well to avoid those expressions which are inappropriate to our language. However, let those who are able to judge this, judge fairly. I have nowhere altered the thoughts of the author, since I consider this to be inexcusable in a translator.

If the reading of this translation gives the Russian lovers of literature an adequate understanding of Shakespeare, if it brings them pleasure, then the translator will be rewarded for his labor. However, he has prepared himself for the opposite. But will not the one be more pleasant for him than the other? —Perhaps.

1786–87

---

to *Julius Caesar* for his introduction. The original of his quote from the "French translators" (Le Tourneur) is as follows: "Brutus . . . est l'être moral le plus rare, le plus sublime et le plus intéressant. Antoine a dit de lui, *voilà un homme:* Shakespeare en nous le retraçant a pu dire, *voilà un caractère;* c'est en effet le plus beau qui jamais'ait été mis sur le scène" (II, 380).

What Does the Writer Need?

IT IS SAID that a writer needs talent and knowledge: a sharp, penetrating mind, a lively imagination, and so on. This is true: but it is not all. He must possess in addition a good, tender heart if he wants to be the friend and favorite of our soul; if he wants his endowments to shine with a steady light; if he wants to write for eternity and collect the benedictions of people. The creator is always depicted in his creation and frequently—against his will. The hypocrite tries in vain to deceive his readers and to conceal his hard heart beneath the gilded dress of pompous words; he speaks to us in vain of

161

mercy, compassion, virtue! All his outcries are cold, soulless, lifeless; and the nourishing, ethereal flame never pours from his creations into the tender soul of the reader.

Had heaven provided some monster with the great endowments of the famous Arouet,† then, instead of the beautiful *Zaïre,* he would have written a caricature of *Zaïre.* The purest salubrious nectar becomes a vile, poisonous drink in a filthy vessel.

If you want to paint your portrait, then look first into the faithful mirror: Can your face be a subject of art, which must be concerned with the beautiful, depict beauty, harmony, and diffuse pleasant impressions in the *area of the emotional?* If creative nature fashioned you in an hour of carelessness or in a moment of conflict with beauty: then be sensible, do not misuse the artist's brush—forsake your intention. You take up the pen and you want to be an author: Then ask yourself, alone, without witnesses, sincerely: *What sort of a person am I?* for you want to paint the portrait of your soul and heart.

Do you really think that Gessner [1] could have depicted so charmingly the innocence and natural goodness of his shepherds and shepherdesses if these attractive traits were alien to his own heart?

You want to be an author: Read the history of the misfortunes of the human race—and if your heart is not suffused with blood, forsake your pen—or it will depict the cold gloom of your soul.

But if all the grief-laden, all the oppressed, all the weeping find a path to your sensitive breast; if your soul can rise to

† The defender and protector of the innocent, the benefactor of the Calas family, the benefactor of all the Ferney inhabitants did not have, of course, an evil heart.

1. Salomon Gessner (1730–88), a Swiss poet of idylls which were very popular in Russia. See the Introduction for a discussion of the idyllic tradition in Russia and Karamzin's strictures upon it.

a *passion for the good,* can nourish within itself a sacred *desire for the general welfare,* unrestricted by any limits, then boldly invoke the Parnassian goddesses—they will pass by the magnificent palaces and visit your humble cottage—you will not be a useless writer—and none of the virtuous will look with dry eyes on your grave.

Style, figures of speech, metaphors, images, locutions—all these touch and captivate us when they are animated by feeling; if it does not excite the imagination of the writer, then never will my tears, never will my smile, be his reward.

Why does Jean-Jacques Rousseau please us with all his frailties and errors? Why do we love to read him even when he daydreams or entangles himself in contradictions?—Because sparks of his passionate love of humanity flash through his very errors; because his very frailties manifest a certain sweet natural goodness.

In contradistinction to this, many other authors, despite their learning and knowledge, disturb my spirit even when they speak the truth: because in their mouths this truth is dead; because this truth flows not from a virtuous heart; because the breath of love does not warm it.

In a word: I am convinced that a bad man cannot be a good author.

1794

Preface

to the Second Book

of Aonides

THE FIRST BOOK of *Aonides* was well received (if I am not mistaken) by lovers of Russian poetry; exactly a year later the second appears—its fate depends upon the public.[1]

"Why, among the many good poems published in *Aonides*, are there some . . . far from perfect, weak . . . or whatever you want to call them?"

Partly to encourage immature talents who might mature and, with the passing of time, produce something excellent; partly that the just criticism of the public might compel us to

1. The title of this article has been supplied.

write with greater care; that readers might be pleased to see how our young poets year by year refine their taste and style; and, finally, that the presence of the *not very good* might raise all the more the *good*. In a word, *Aonides* must demonstrate the state of our poetry, its beauties and deficiencies.

Without violating the confidence of my dear collaborators, without violating the prerogatives of a publisher, I shall venture only to note the two major defects of our young muses: an excessive pomposity, an inappropriate thunder of words, and, frequently, a feigned lachrymosity.†

Poetry consists not in the inflated descriptions of terrible scenes of nature but in the vivacity of thoughts and feelings. If the poet writes not about that which really interests his soul; if he is not the slave but the tyrant of his imagination, forcing it to pursue alien, remote, unfamiliar ideas; if he describes not those objects which are close to him and by their own power attract his imagination; if he constrains himself or only imitates another (which is all the same)—then in his works there will never be any vivacity, truth, or that conformity of parts which forms a whole and without which any poem (even despite its many felicitous phrases) is similar to that strange being described by Horace in the beginning of his epistle to the Pisos.[2] It is better for the young nursling of the

† I am not speaking at all about incorrect rhymes, although to achieve perfection, poetic rhyme must be correct.

2. Gn. Calpurnius Piso (?), consul in 23 B.C., and his two sons. Karamzin is referring here to the "Art of Poetry," the first lines of which in the translation of Smith Palmer Bovie are as follows:

> Suppose you'd been asked to come for a private view
> Of a painting wherein the artist had chosen to join
> To a human head the neck of a horse, and gone on
> To collect some odds and ends of arms and legs
> And plaster the surface with feathers of differing colors,
> So that what began as a lovely woman at the top
> Tapered off into a slimy, discolored fish—
> Could you keep from laughing, my friends?

Muses to depict in poetry the first impressions of love, friendship, the delicate beauties of nature, rather than the destruction of the world, a general conflagration of nature,† and so on in this fashion.

One must not think that only lofty subjects can excite a poet and serve to demonstrate his gifts: on the contrary, the true poet finds the poetic side in the most ordinary things; it is his business to present everything in living colors, to attach to everything a witty thought, a delicate feeling, or to adorn the ordinary thought, the ordinary feeling, with an expression that shows the nuances hidden from other people's eyes, to find the imperceptible analogies, similarities, to play with ideas and like Jupiter (as the sage, Aesop, said of him) sometimes *to make the small, great,* and, sometimes, *to make the great, small.* Only *bombast,* only the thunder of words, nearly deafens us and never reaches the heart; contrary to this, a delicate thought, a fine stroke of the imagination or feeling, acts immediately on the soul of the reader; the wise poem is engraved in the memory, the thunderous poem is forgotten.

Nor is it also necessary to speak incessantly of tears, modifying them with different epithets, terming them gleaming and diamond-like—this *method of affecting* is very unreliable: it is necessary to describe their cause in a striking fashion; to denote grief not only by its *general* features—which, since they are quite ordinary, cannot produce a strong reaction in the heart of a reader—but by its *special features,* which are related to the character and circumstances of the poet. These very features, these details, and this, so to speak, personality assure us of the truth of the descriptions and often deceive us; but such deception is the triumph of art.

† A composition entitled "The End of the Worlds" was sent to the editor; it seemed to him too horrible for *Aonides.*

It is difficult, difficult to be an absolutely good writer both in poetry and prose; but then much honor goes to the conqueror of the difficulties (because the art of writing is, of course, the first and the most renowned, demanding a rare perfection of one's spiritual abilities); but then a nation is honored by its authors; but then the preeminence of a nation is judged by the success of its authors. In all fairness to the taste and enlightenment of our dear countrymen, I deem it unnecessary to demonstrate here the use and importance of literature, which, since it generally influences the pleasant side of life, social intercourse, and the perfection of language (which is indissolubly connected with the intellectual and moral perfection of every people), is always more useful, more pleasant, for those who practice it: It occupies, consoles them in rural isolation; it attunes their soul to a deep feeling for the beauties of nature and to those delicate desires for morality which will always be the chief source of earthly bliss; it provides the friendship of the best people or serves, itself, in place of a friend. Who in our times could be its enemy? No one, of course. But Voltaire says,

If there are in our very civilized nation some barbarians and some ignoramuses who dare to disapprove of such an honorable occupation, then one can rest assured that they would do the same if they were able. I am quite convinced that when a man does not cultivate his talent, it is that he does not have any; that there is no man who would not write poetry if he had been born a poet, who would not compose music if he had been born a musician.[3]

1797

3. Karamzin has quoted from the penultimate paragraph of Voltaire's "Lettre à M. Cideville sur 'Le Temple du Goût,'" April 12, 1733. The entire paragraph follows: "Il me reste à dire un mot sur notre jeune noblesse, que emploie l'heureux loisir de la paix à cultiver les lettres et les arts; bien différente en cela des augustes

Visigoths, leurs ancêtres, qui ne savaient pas signer leurs noms. S'il
y a encore dans notre nation si polie quelques barbares et quelques
mauvais plaisants qui osent désapprouver des occupations si estim-
ables, on peut assurer qu'ils en feraient autant s'ils le pouvaient. Je
suis très-persuadé que quand un homme ne cultive point un talent,
c'est qu'il ne l'a pas; qu'il n'y a personne qui ne fît des vers s'il était
né poète, et de la musique s'il était né musicien."

My Confession:

A Letter to an Editor

of a Journal

I PROFESS TO YOU, dear sir, that I do not read your journal, but I wish that you would publish my letter in it. Why? I don't know myself. I have lived for more than forty years in this world and never yet have held myself accountable either for my wishes or for my acts. The great words "So be it" were always my motto.

I intend to speak about myself: I took it into my head and wrote—my own confession, never considering whether it would please the readers or not. The present century can be called a century of *frankness* in a physical and moral sense: Look at our sweet beauties! At one time people hid in dark homes and behind a shield of tall fences. Now, everywhere, homes are bright and their large windows face the street; we invite observation! We want to live, act, and think through a transparent glass. Today people travel not to understand and describe other lands faithfully but to get the chance to chatter about themselves; today every writer of a novel hurries to communicate as soon as possible his own manner of thought on important and unimportant issues. In addition to this, how many books come out with the titles: *My Experiences, A Secret Journal of My Heart!* What's the pen for, if not for a sincere profession? The sooner man loses his old-fashioned barbaric sense of shame, then it will be all the easier to become the author of a confession. Here it is not necessary to rack one's brains; it is only necessary to recall one's pranks, and the book is ready.

However, don't think that I want to justify myself through precedents; no, such an idea offends my self-esteem. I only trace my own performance and in passing note that in a certain way it corresponds to the general; but God preserve me from appearing to be a slavish imitator! Therefore, contrary to all confessors, I state in advance that my professions have no moral purpose whatsoever. I write—so be it! I differ in still another respect from my brethren—the authors, to wit —in brevity. They know how to spawn multitudes from nothing; I shall describe the most important events of my life on a small sheet.

I shall begin with the assurance that nature had produced in me a completely unique individual and that fate has stamped all the events of my life with some sort of special seal. For example, I was born the son of a rich, aristocratic gentleman —and grew up a scamp! I committed all sorts of pranks—and was never thrashed! I learned French—and didn't know my own language! At ten, I acted in the theater—and at fifteen, had no idea of the duties of a man and a citizen.

In my sixteenth year, I was given a fairly good rank and, without being told the reason, was sent abroad. It is true that a tutor went with me, a Genevan (please note, not a Frenchman because at this time French governors were already going out of style in our aristocratic homes), who had been given all the necessary instructions. Mr. Mendel knew what an aristocratic young man is chiefly trained for and most of all he knew what was expedient for himself—and treated me in accord with his own, wise plan. One must be fair to him: he loved sincerity and quickly came to an understanding with me. "Dear Count," my tutor said to me.—"Nature and fate have arranged to make you a model of amiability and happiness; you are handsome, intelligent, rich, and aristocratic; sufficient for a brilliant role in the world! Everything else is not worth your labor. We are going to the University of Leipzig; your parents, as is customary, wish you to adorn your mind with learning and they have entrusted you to my care; be at ease! I was born in a republic and hate tyranny! I hope only that my indulgence will in time merit your thankfulness." I embraced him and promised him such a pension as not even a minister always receives after many years' service.

When we arrived in Leipzig, we hastened to make the acquaintance of all the famous professors—and the nymphs. My tutor had a great respect for the former and a slight weakness for the latter. I took him for my model—and for one we gave dinners, for the others—suppers. The hours of the lectures seemed minutes because I loved to doze beneath the rostrum of the doctors, and could not really enjoy listening to them because I never listened. Meanwhile, Mr. Mendel informed my parents every week of the great accomplishments of their dear son and filled entire pages with the names of sciences which I was being taught.

Finally, after we had spent three years in Leipzig, we began to travel, having hired a secretary to describe the interesting sights because Mr. Mendel was lazy. My parents received a heavy packet from every town; they could not delight enough in the intelligent observations of their son and read them with pride to our relatives. I was not responsible for a single line, since I had authorized my secretary to philosophize in my place (fortunately, his handwriting was just the same as mine), but I added to some of his descriptions my own expressive caricatures—the product of the only talent which nature had given me!

However, I caused quite a furor in my travels—while dancing quadrilles with prominent women of the German princely courts, I deliberately dropped them on the floor in a most indecorous manner; but more important than this, while kissing the slipper of the Pope among the good Catholics, I bit his foot and forced the poor old gent to cry out at the top of his lungs. This joke did not pass without cost, and I had to sit several days in the fortress of Sant' Angelo. My customary amusement on the road was—to shoot paper pellets from an air pistol at the backs of the postilions!

In Paris I associated with many of the famous cutups and I found that I could astound them by my audacious philosophy as well as by all the subtleties of a rake's language, by all its technical expressions, which were borrowed for the most part from Mr. Mendel, who had served at one time as the personal secretary of the Duc de Richelieu. Introduced into several good homes, I also got the chance to know the most famous French wits; once I heard a reading of La Harpe's *Mélanie,* I praised the talent of the author without stint, and later found out that he, in a letter to one aristocratic gentleman in P*, described me (undoubtedly out of gratitude) as a rare young man, born to honor and glorify the fatherland. I had the good fortune to be presented to the Duc d'Orléans, to sup with his select friends and to share their amusements, which were worthy of the brush of a new Petronius.

It was necessary to see England; like Alcibiades, I became a different man in a different country and drank so heartily with the Britons that in a month I had to take to bed. Taking advantage of the period of recuperation, I drew caricatures of the entire royal family—and the London journals praised them highly.

The return of my strength was a grievous thing for Mr. Mendel: I took it into my head to knock him off the ladder because he took it into his head to snuggle up to my Jeannie. The tender English girl swooned while my tutor counted the rungs with his head. However, I assure the reader that my heart was quite incapable of jealousy: this passing action was, of course, a consequence of my illness. Mr. Mendel parted with me. We both informed my parents of our break; he called me a scamp and I described him as unworthy of the name of tutor. Both the former and the latter judgment could be deemed correct, but Mama believed only me and Papa agreed with her.

Finally, I returned to my fatherland, where laurels and myrtles awaited me. There was not a single clear idea in my head, and in my heart—no strong emotion except boredom. All the world seemed to me the indiscriminate pattern of a Chinese screen, all rules—a bridle for weak minds, all duties —an intolerable restraint. The attentions of my parents made no impression on my cold soul; but, aware of the advantages accruing to a man educated in foreign lands, I hastened to impress through various oddities the minds of my fellow countrymen and, happily, saw myself become the real legislator of the capital. A seafarer does not watch his magnetic needle so attentively during a storm as young people watched me so that they might imitate me in everything. Everywhere, as in a mirror, I saw myself from head to toe: all my actions were copied and repeated quite faithfully. This amused me exceedingly. But women were my main object; their adulatory attention opened a vast sphere of activity for me. Here I cannot restrain myself from several philosophical observations.

Amorousity—pardon the new word; it expresses the thing —amorousity, I say, is a most beneficent invention for the world, for without it the world would be like a Trappist monastery. But with it, young people can occupy the emptiness of their lives in a most beautiful fashion. When you open your eyes, you know what to think about; when you appear in society, you know whom to seek with your eyes; everything has its purpose. It is true that husbands are sometimes annoyed; that wives sometimes make fools of themselves out of jealousy; but we are occupied—and this is the chief thing! On the one hand, the art of pleasing, on the other—the art of dissembling and deceiving one's self, all this does not allow the heart to doze off. Frequently, families are upset, but this has its own charm. Scenes of fainting, despair, are beautiful to the connoisseur. *Sauve qui peut,* let everyone think of himself— and it is sufficient!

As a fashionable charmer, I had the good fortune to cause arguments among many intimate female friends and more than one wife to part with her husband. Every tale of seduction brought me greater and greater glory. Horrible things were said about my character: this, in itself, excited a curiosity which affects the feminine heart in a lively and strong fashion. My system of love was most reliable; I tyrannized women now with indifference, now with jealousy; not before ten in the evening did I take up my *amorous watch;* I seated myself on an ottoman, I yawned, I sniffed Hoffman's drops or began to praise another woman; secret annoyance, reproaches, tears diverted me for some six weeks, sometimes for much longer; finally the end of the liaison followed—and a new myrtle garland fell on my head. Justice demands my profession that not all the beauties became my Didos; no, one of them, losing patience, dared to show me the door. I was desperate—and on the next day I depicted her in a striking caricature: I compelled everyone to laugh and was consoled.

Suddenly I thought of marriage, not only to please my mother (my father was no longer with us) but to set up in my home a noble's theater, which would serve as a pleasant distraction amid the difficult obligations of a fashionable man. I chose a beautiful maid of modest means (well-educated in an aristocratic home), hoping that out of gratitude she would leave me in peace, and with these ideas in mind I promised to sup on the next day, as usual alone, with the frolicsome Alina, who was then keeping me busy with her favors. Things turned out quite the opposite. Out of gratitude Emilia considered it her duty to be a tender, passionate wife, and tenderness and passion are always jealous. My philosophy made her weep, flare up: I armed myself with patience, watched, listened calmly; I played with her shawl—and yawned, figuring that heavy storms do not last long, especially those of a woman. Actually, Emilia gradually came to her senses, calmed down, and became far sweeter; her languid glances perked up, and her petty reproaches were spoken softly, even with a smile. Finally, I was completely convinced of my wife's reform when I saw her surrounded by a crowd of admirers. Our home was consequently far more pleasant. Emilia stopped insulting the young women and tried in every possible way to merit the name of an amiable mistress. We recruited Italian *castrate*, performed operas, comedies, gave small balls, larger suppers —we signed bills and never counted the amount—we borrowed money and never had any—in short, we lived beautifully!

Only my mother, whose temperament had been spoiled by old age, was upset and often reproached me for foolish imprudence; she said that we were ruining ourselves; she even said that Emilia acted immorally! But I—yawned and, as a good son should, advised her to take care of her health, that is, not to get angry. She did not want to listen to me and passed away before her time. Poor thing! We felt sorry for her—and sincerely so, since her death put an end to our plays for several months.

Minor complications soon appeared in our household affairs: sometimes immediately before a large supper party the butler would tell me that he did not have a ruble for expenses and that he could not borrow money anywhere. In such a case, I usually chased him out of the room—and the supper turned out beautifully. Kind people appeared with their wares: some made their sales on the basis of promissory notes, others instantly bought them for cold cash and that was that. But from time to time greater difficulties were encountered, and frequently for a promissory note of a thousand rubles I was given only some six dozen pomades! I must inform my reader that those clever people, whom the profane call usurers, know all the needs and all the commercial resources of our rich wastrels by heart; taking their pencil in hand, they instantly calculate in how many years, months, days, and hours so-and-so will not have a penny to his name; by this true reckoning they serve their neighbor energetically, zealously, and rarely do they make a mistake. Sooner than all the others, our homegrown moneymongers abandon a man on the glorious and broad path of ruination, like melancholy doctors who condemn their patients to death much too soon; they surrender him to the hands of the foreign usurers: the Germans give way to the French, the French—to the Italians, the Italians—to the Greeks; in this last stage the ruble of the wastrel is only worth a kopeck. I calmly passed through all the Jews' stalls and stood now on the last rung. My estate was inventoried, sold at a public auction, but I still did not despair and the very day they drove me from my home I thought of playing the leading role in the comedy *The Unconcerned*. The cruel moneylenders did not want to see the play—and I had to seek refuge in the home of a relative.

If the reader is amazed that seven or eight thousand souls evaporated so quickly, like smoke, then he undoubtedly does not know the multiplicative force of debts, which are calculated not by the debtor but by the moneylenders; promissory notes, like polyps, propagate in a miraculous fashion if the curtain of unconcern hides the consequences from the eyes of reason. Furthermore, every honorable wastrel can find trustworthy cohorts among his stewards and butlers, who in every possible way ease the burden of the master's estate, having observed that this oppresses the master.—I have termed the wastrel honorable, and hasten to justify myself. He is a benefactor of the fatherland and the people, since he shares his wealth with society. The moneygrubber is like a thirsty river which flows in a straight line, engulfs brooklets and streams, moistens only its own banks, and desiccates the adjacent lands, but the spendthrift can be compared to a bounteous river, which divides itself into a thousand branches, brings moisture to a great expanse of land, and, disappearing gradually, becomes a sacrifice to its own beneficence.

He who wants to can imagine me walking along the street calmly and even proudly; behind me, two servants carry two baskets, crammed with women's love letters: the only treasure which the moneylenders allowed me to carry from my home! My relative received me coldly and reproachfully. Emilia arrived at his place soon after me and, oblivious to the fact that we both had squandered the estate, hurled bitter accusations at me, announced triumphantly that our union was shattered, entered her carriage, and disappeared. I flew to the woman who just a day before had assured me of her love—I was not admitted; I flew to my innumerable friends; some were not at home, others took it upon themselves to read bookish admonitions to me from memory, to the effect that one must be moderate and judicious in life! They should have spoken thus when I regaled them with wine and food.—To top it all, I was thrown out of the service as a dissolute individual.

Such incidents and disappointments might have embittered another, but I was born a philosopher—I endured everything calmly and repeated my favorite words: "A Chinese screen! A Chinese screen!" Worst of all, the moneylenders, dissatisfied with the residue of my estate, threatened to clap me in prison. I confess that the idea of a dark hole shook even my philosophy.

After some two months, a rich prince came to me, demanded that I sign some paper, and promised to satisfy my creditors; that is, I had to be a party to a fraud which gave Emilia the right to choose another husband. At first I burst out laughing, and then thought it over, imagining, on the one hand, the terrors of the black hole, and on the other—the evil gibes of people. Meanwhile, the prince spoke of his gratitude, confessed that he intended to marry Emilia, wishing to save her from the afflictions of poverty, offered me his friendship, assured me that his home would be my home, and even invited me to live there. Here a *happy thought* entered my head: I signed the paper.

In an eloquent letter to me, Emilia expressed her thankfulness (she married the prince, who immediately redeemed my promissory notes) and in conclusion said: "We could not be happy as husband and wife: at least we shall be tender friends! My husband has vowed to love you as a brother." I hastened to assure her of my sensitivity—and from that time on, I settled down at the prince's, dined, supped with Emilia, appeared languid, sad, and, when left alone with her, spoke tearfully of my previous imprudence, of my heartfelt repentance, of my happiness, forever lost, that is, as the spouse of the

most lovable woman in the world. She joked at first but
gradually began to hear me out with a grave face and to
become pensive. One should know that the prince was elderly
and of an extremely unpleasant appearance. Her eyes often
compared us quietly and she would lower them with a sad
expression. Emilia had loved me once; now that I was no
longer her husband, I seemed all the more lovable to her.
Since she was afraid of society, which had loudly condemned
her second marriage, she led a solitary life; solitude, as is
known, feeds the passions. A woman, the most romantic, can
be tempted by wealth in certain situations, but wealth loses all
its value at the first stirring of the heart. I do not want to bore
the reader with lengthy preliminaries. *My plan* was carried out
successfully. We understood each other. Emilia surrendered
herself to me with every indication of a most vivacious passion, while for a moment I could scarcely restrain my laughter
in imagining the oddity of my victory and the novelty of such
a liaison.—The old husband had taken revenge on the new,
but I was still not satisfied with Emilia's rapture, the secret
assignations, the tender letters: I wanted resounding glory! I
proposed that my wife-mistress go away with me. She was
frightened—she described our situation as most fortunate (because the prince was ashamed to be jealous of me)—foresaw
the revulsion of society if we should venture on such an
incredible course of debauchery—and in tears implored me to
have pity on her lot. But a woman who has already trans-
gressed (in the words of the moralists) against many duties
cannot be responsible for her conduct. I insisted upon it,
demanded, threatened (as I recall) to shoot myself—and in a
few days we found ourselves on the M—w road.

My triumph was complete; I vividly imagined the conster-
nation of the poor prince and of all honorable people; I
compared myself to the romantic Lovelaces and placed them
beneath me: they carried off their mistresses while I carried off

my former wife from her second husband! Emilia was sad but consoled herself with the thought that she was following the stirring of an unconquerable feeling and that her love for me was heroic—a consolation women usually take refuge in when deluded by passion or imagination!

In M—w my aristocratic relatives would not allow me into their homes, while my pious aunts and grandmothers crossed themselves in horror when they met me on the street. On the other hand, several young people were amazed at my audacious actions and accepted me as their hero. I rested on my laurels, unafraid of any consequences: because the good prince, grief locked in his heart, did not complain to anyone and told his friends that he himself had sent his wife to M—w to economize. Emilia sold her diamonds and we lived not badly; but she sometimes complained of my indifference and, finally, after she had discovered that I was having an affair with a famous hussy, took to bed, told me that she could endure my unfaithfulness as my wife but as my mistress it would be her death. Emilia kept her word—and when dying she said things to me that would have made my hair stand on end if, unfortunately, I had had the faintest glimmer of conscience; but I listened coldly and went to sleep calmly; only that night I had a terrible dream, one which, undoubtedly, could not really happen.

I do not want to speak of my further amatory adventures, which are not particularly brilliant, although I still managed to ruin two or three women (it's true, they weren't very young). When I finally realized that the years and lack of restraint had placed their sullen imprint on my face, I decided upon other measures; I became a usurer and, further, a clown, a jester, a confidant of the little weaknesses of husbands and wives. Is it any wonder that entree to many distinguished homes was again made available to me? Such people are necessary in any event. In short, I am satisfied with my position and, since I see the action of inescapable destiny in everything, I have not clouded a single moment of my life with sorrowful repentance. Were I able to bring back the past, I think I would repeat again my every deed: I would like to bite the Pope's foot once more, lead a debauched life in Paris, drink in London, act out amorous comedies in the theater and in society, squander my estate, and carry off my own wife from her second husband. It is true that certain people look upon my life with contempt and say that I have shamed my name, that an aristocrat is obligated to be a useful member of the state and a virtuous citizen of the fatherland. But should I believe them, since I see, on one hand, how many of my amiable compatriots try to imitate me, live without purpose, marry without love, divorce themselves for amusement, and ruin themselves for suppers! No, no! I have fulfilled my predestination, and like a wanderer who, standing on a height, gazes with pleasure on the distance he has traversed, I joyfully remember my past experiences and say to myself: thus have I lived!

Count NN.
1802

On the Book Trade

and Love of Reading

in Russia

TWENTY-FIVE YEARS AGO there were two bookstores in Moscow, the annual sales of which did not amount to 10,000 rubles. Now there are twenty, and together they make an annual profit of about 200,000 rubles. How much then have the lovers of reading increased in Russia? This pleases everyone who desires intellectual progress and knows that love of reading contributes so much to it.

In Moscow Mr. Novikov was the chief promoter of the book trade. After he had leased the University Printing House, he increased the mechanical means of book printing, had books translated, established stores in other towns, in every possible way tried to entice the public to read, ferreted out the general taste and did not forget the individual. He traded books as a rich Dutch or English merchant trades the products of all lands: that is, with intelligence, perspicacity, farsighted understanding. Previously, not more than 600 copies of Moscow newspapers were circulated; Mr. Novikov made them far richer in content, added to the political articles various others, and, finally, distributed with the *Gazette* a free supplement, "Readings for Children," which, despite the schoolboy translations of many pieces, pleased the public with the novelty of its subject and the variety of its material. The number of subscribers increased annually and in some ten years had reached 4,000. From 1797 newspapers became important for Russia because the edicts of His Imperial Majesty and other state proceedings were inserted in them, and now about 6,000 copies of Moscow newspapers are circulated: undoubtedly the number is still small, when we consider the vastness of the empire, but large when compared with the previous circulation; and hardly in any other country has the number of those interested in reading increased so quickly as in Russia. It is true that many noblemen, even those who are well off, still do not take newspapers; but on the other hand, the merchants, the burghers, now love to read them. The poorest people subscribe, even the most illiterate want to find out *what do they write from foreign lands!* One of my acquaintances happened to see several pastry cooks standing around a reader and listening very attentively to a description of a battle between the Austrians and the French. He inquired and discovered that five of them had pooled their money and taken the Moscow newspapers, although four of them could not read; but the fifth deciphered the letters while the others listened.

Our book trade cannot yet be compared with the German, French, or English; but what can we not expect from it in time, considering its annual progress? Now in almost all provincial towns there are bookstores: the riches of our literature, together with other wares, are delivered to every fair. Thus, for example, the rural noblewomen at the St. Macarius Fair lay in not only a supply of bonnets but also of books. Previously, the hucksters passed through the villages with ribbons and rings; today they go with scholarly wares, and although for the most part they do not know how to read, nonetheless, in an attempt to attract dilettantes, they relate the contents of the novels and comedies, of course, in their own fashion and quite amusingly. I know noblemen whose annual income is not more than 500 rubles, but they collect, in their words, "little libraries," take delight in them, and, while we throw around expensive editions of Voltaire, Buffon, they will not let a speck of dust fall on *Miramond;* [1] they read each book several times and reread them with new pleasure.

The curious would, perhaps, like to know what type of book is sold most among us? I have inquired about this of many booksellers, and everyone, without hesitation, answered: "Novels!" It is no wonder: this type of writing undoubtedly captivates a larger portion of the public, engaging the heart and imagination, picturing the world and people, who are similar to us, in interesting situations, depicting the most powerful and at the same time the most common passion in its varied activities. Not everyone can philosophize or take the place of the heroes of history; but everyone loves, has loved, or wants to love, and finds in the romantic hero his own self. It seems to the reader that the author speaks to him in the language of his own heart; in one novel he nourishes hope, in another—a pleasant recollection. In this type of book, as is

---

1. *Inconstant Fortune, or the Adventures of Miramond* ("Nepostoiannaia Fortuna, ili Pokhozhdenie Miramonda") a *roman d'aventure* by F. A. Emin (1735?–70) published in 1763.

known, we have more translated than original works and, consequently, foreign authors have surpassed the fame of the Russians. Now, Kotzebue [2] is terribly fashionable—and as the Parisian booksellers at one time demanded *Lettres persanes* [3] from every writer, so our booksellers demand from the translators and the authors themselves Kotzebue, only Kotzebue!! A novel, a tale, good or bad—it is all the same, if on the title page there is the name of the famous Kotzebue!

I do not know about others, but I am happy so long as they read. And novels, the most mediocre—even written without any talent—contribute in some way to enlightenment. He who is captivated by *Nikanor, the Ill-fated Nobleman*, [4] stands somewhat beneath the author on the ladder of intellectual development, and does well in reading this novel: because, without any doubt, he learns something of ideas and their expression. As soon as there is a great distance between the author and the reader, then the former cannot greatly influence the latter, however intelligent he might be. They must be a little closer to each other: one, to Jean-Jacques, the other, to *Nikanor*. As physical taste generally informs us of the food that meets our needs, so moral taste reveals to man the true similarity of an object with his soul; but the soul can ascend

2. August F. F. von Kotzebue (1761–1819), the author of several highly popular plays, the most famous of which are *Menschenhass und Reue* (1787) and *Die deutschen Kleinstädter* (1803).

3. A satire on political and ecclesiastical conditions in France; published by Montesquieu in 1721, it became very popular in Russia as one of the sources for the dissemination of the ideas of the French Enlightenment.

4. *The Ill-fated Nikanor, or the Adventures in the Life of a Russian Nobleman* ("Neschastnyi Nikanor, ili Prikliuchenie zhizni rossiiskogo dvorianina"), an anonymous novel, combining the features of the rudimentary realistic novel of the century with those of the adventure novel; published in 1795.

gradually—and he who begins with the *Ill-fated Nobleman* often reaches as far as Grandison.[5]

All pleasurable reading influences the mind, without which the heart cannot feel, nor the imagination conceive. In very bad novels there is still a certain logic and rhetoric: He who reads them will speak better and more coherently than the utter ignoramus who has never opened a book in his life. Furthermore, contemporary novels are rich in all types of information. An author, having taken it upon himself to write three or four volumes, resorts to every expediency, and even to all branches of knowledge, to fill them: Now he describes some kind of American island, depleting Büsching; now he explains the characteristics of local plants, consulting Bomare; thus, the reader learns both geography and natural history; and I am sure that soon in some kind of German novel the new planet of Piazzi will be described in greater detail than in the *Petersburg Gazette!* [6]

It is unjust to believe that novels can harm the heart: they all, usually, represent the glory of virtue or an edifying consequence. It is true that certain characters in them are both

5. The hero of Richardson's novel, *History of Sir Charles Grandison*, 1754.

6. Anton Friedrich Büsching (1724–93), German geographer, whose principal work was *Neue Erdbeschreibung*, 1754–92. Although his interests cover a wide variety of fields, he is chiefly known as the founder of political geography. Jacques-Christophe Valmont de Bomare (1731–1807), French naturalist, who through his public courses and writings helped popularize the young science of natural history in the eighteenth century. His most important work is the *Dictionnaire Raisonné Universel d'Histoire Naturelle*, 1765. Giuseppe Piazzi (1746–1826), Italian astronomer, who discovered a new planet on January 1, 1801, quite by chance. Perhaps in recognition of the fortuitous circumstances, he modestly refused to name it after himself and chose instead the name Ceres, after the ancient goddess of Sicily.

attractive and depraved; but in what way precisely are they attractive? Through certain good characteristics, with which the author colors over their blackness: consequently good triumphs even in evil itself. Our moral nature is such that the heart is not satisfied by the depiction of bad people and will never make them its favorites. What novels are most popular? Usually, sentimental: tears, shed by the reader, always flow from a love of goodness and nourish it. No, no! Bad people do not even read novels. Their cruel souls are not susceptible to the gentle impressions of love and cannot be interested in the fate of tenderness. The vilely selfish, the egoist, can he find himself in the charming romantic hero? What need does he have for others? It is indisputable that novels make both the heart and the imagination . . . *romantic:* What's the harm? In a certain sense it is so much the better for us, inhabitants of the cold and iron north! Undoubtedly, it is not romantic hearts who are the cause of that evil in the world about which we hear complaints from all sides, but the coarse and cold, that is, quite the opposite! The romantic heart causes itself more grief than others; but, then, it loves this grief and will not give it up for the very pleasures of the egoists.

In a word, it is good that our public also reads novels.

1802

Why Is There
So Little Writing Talent
in Russia?

WERE WE TO POSE THIS QUESTION to a foreigner, especially a Frenchman, then he, without too much thought, would answer: "Because of the cold climate." From the time of Montesquieu, all phenomena of the intellectual, political, and moral world have been explained by the climate.[1] "Ah, mon

1. Charles de Sécondat (1689–1755), Baron de la Brède et de Montesquieu, wrote *De l'esprit des lois* in 1748. One of the theses of the book is that climate has a determining influence on a people's passions and character. This idea became exceedingly popular in the writing of the latter part of the century. Montesquieu does not say

cher Monsieur, n'avez vous le nez gelé?" said Diderot in Petersburg to one of his countrymen, who had complained that his great mind was not appreciated in Russia and who had some days before actually frozen his nose slightly.

But Moscow is not Kamchatka, not Lapland; the sun is just as bright here as it is in other lands; here also there are spring and summer, flowers and greenery. It is true that we have a more extensive cold season; but can its effect, so moderated in Russia by the protective means which have been devised, be detrimental to man's endowments? Even the question seems ridiculous! Rather heat, in debilitating the nerves (the immediate contact of the soul), diminishes that force of thought and imagination which makes up talent. It has long been apparent to medical observers that inhabitants of the north live longer than the inhabitants of the south: the climate, beneficial to the physical constitution, undoubtedly, is not injurious to the activities of the soul, which is so closely connected to the body in this world.—If a hot climate could produce talents of the mind, then in the Archipelago pure incense would always burn to the Muses, and in Italy Virgils and Tassos would sing; but in the Archipelago they burn . . . tobacco, and in Italy *castrate* . . . sing.

There is, of course, less writing talent among us than among other European people; but we have had, do have, it, and consequently nature has not condemned us to admire it only in foreign lands. It is not in our climate but in the circumstances of Russian civil life that one must seek an answer to the question: "Why are good writers rare among us?"

Although talent is an inspiration of nature, still it must be

---

that the influence of climate is such that no human control is possible but, rather, that man should adapt himself to climatic conditions in the formation of his government and laws.

uncovered by study and matured in constant practice. The author has to possess not only a properly called endowment —that is, some sort of special faculty derived from his spiritual capacities—but also much historical information, a logically trained mind, fine taste, and a knowledge of society. How much time must be spent just to master completely the spirit of one's own language? Voltaire has justly observed that in six years one can learn all the major languages but that one must study one's native tongue an entire lifetime. It is even more difficult for us Russians than for the others. A Frenchman, having read Montaigne, Pascal, five or six authors of the age of Louis XIV, Voltaire, Rousseau, Thomas,[2] Marmontel,† can understand perfectly all the variations of his own language; but we, having read many ecclesiastical and secular books, will pick up only the material or verbal wealth of the language, the soul and beauties of which are created by the artist. True writers are still so few among us that they have not succeeded in creating models in many genres; they have not succeeded in enriching our vocabulary with subtle ideas; they have not shown how one must express pleasantly certain, rather ordinary, thoughts. The Russian *candidate for the writing profession,* dissatisfied with books, ought to close them and listen to the conversations about him in order to understand his language more completely. Here is a new calamity: French is more common in our better homes! Our sweet women, whose conversation should be caught to adorn a novel or a comedy with attractive, happy expressions, captivate us with non-Russian sentences. What then should an author do? To make up, to compose the expressions; to divine the best choice of words; to give some new twist to the old; to present them in a new

2. Antoine-Léonard Thomas (1732–85), a minor writer of the *philosophe* school and a member of the French Academy.

† As the author of the unique tales.

association, but so skillfully as to deceive the readers and conceal from them the uncommonness of the expression! Is it any wonder that the writers of certain Russian comedies and novels have not surmounted this great obstacle and that society women do not have the patience to hear or read them, since they have found that people of taste do not speak in that way? If you ask them: "How, then, should one speak?" then any one of them would answer: "I do not know; but this is crude, intolerable!"—In a word, the French language is entirely in books (with all its colors and shadows, as in beautiful pictures), but the Russian is only partly so; the French write as they speak but the Russians still have to speak of many subjects as a man of talent would write.

Buffon explained the characteristic of a great talent or genius in a strange way, saying that it is *patience to an extraordinary degree.* But if we ponder this well, we cannot but agree with him; at least without a rare patience genius cannot shine in all its radiance. *Work is the requisite of art;* the desire and capability to conquer difficulties characterize talent. Buffon and J.-J. Rousseau captivate us with their strong and beautiful style: we know from them what the palm of eloquence cost them!

Now I ask: who among us would do battle with a great obstacle to become a good author, if even the most happy endowment possesses a hard crust which can only be rubbed smooth by constant labor? Who among us can burrow in books for ten, twenty years, be an observer, a perpetual student, write and cast his writings into the fire so that something better might rise from the ashes? In Russia, nobles study more than others; but for how long? Until fifteen years of age: then it is time to enter the service, time to seek rank, the most trustworthy way to obtain respect. We are only beginning to love reading; the name of a good writer still does not have the value it does in other lands; when the occasion requires it, one must stake a different claim to a smile of courtesy and kindness. Furthermore the pursuit of rank does not interfere with balls, suppers, celebrations; but a writer's life favors frequent solitude. The young people of the middle social level, who study, are also *in a great haste* to leave school or university in order to get their rewards for their scholarly successes in the civil or military services; but those few who continue their studies rarely have the opportunity to know society—without which it is difficult for a writer to form his own taste, however learned he might be. All the French writers, who serve as models of subtlety and pleasantness, *do correct,* so to say, their academic rhetoric in society, by observing what pleases it and why. It is true that as a school for writers it can also be a grave for endowments: it bestows taste but infringes upon industriousness, which is necessary for great and lasting successes. Happy is he who, when he hears the Sirens, imitates their magical melodies but is able to withdraw when he so desires! Otherwise we are left only with couplets and madrigals. It is necessary to look in upon the social world—absolutely necessary at least during some years—but to live in the study.

In time there will obviously be better authors in Russia—then we shall see among our worldly people more learned ones, or among our learned people—more worldly ones. Talent is now formed among us by chance. Nature and character sometimes oppose the force of circumstances and lead a man along a path which he would not have chosen for the sake of a common good or from which fate would have removed him: thus, Lomonosov [3] was born a peasant and became a famous poet. A proclivity for literature, the sciences, the arts is, undoubtedly, innate since it is always revealed early in life,

3. Mikhail Vasilevich Lomonosov (1711–65) was an outstanding poet of the eighteenth century. In addition to his contributions to Russian literature, he was active in the fields of chemistry, geography, mathematics, mineralogy, and physics.

before the mind is able to apply it to its own material gain. The child who draws charcoal heads on all the walls does not realize as yet that the pictorial arts can bring profits to a man in his life. Another, hearing poetry for the first time, discards his toy and wants to speak in rhyme. What good writer, already in his youth, has not composed satires, songs, novels? But circumstances do not always yield to nature; if they are not favorable to her, then her endowments for the most part die out. What comes into being with difficulty, rarely occurs —however it does occur—and the sensitive heart, the vivacity of thoughts, the activity of the imagination, despite other more apparent or more immediate advantages, sometimes confine a man to his quiet study and compel him to discover inexplicable charms in the labors of the mind, in the development of concepts, in the painting of emotions, in the adornment of language. He thinks—since he wants to bestow a value on his efforts for his own sake—he thinks, I say, that his labor is not without use to his fatherland; that authors help their compatriots *to think and speak better;* that all great people have loved and do love talent; that the Greeks, Romans, French, English, Germans would not have been famed for their minds had they not been famed for their talents; that the dignity of a people is demeaned by the absurdity and inarticulateness of bad writers; that their barbaric taste is a satire on the taste of the people; that models of noble Russian eloquence are hardly less valuable than those very classes of Latin elocution where Cicero and Virgil are interpreted; that it [the author's labor], in selecting patriotic and moral subjects, can benefit manners and nourish a love for the fatherland.—Others may think differently of literature; we do not want to argue with them now.

1802

The Emotional
and the Cold:
Two Characters

THE SPIRIT OF A SYSTEM leads reasonable people to assert many strange and even absurd things: Thus, some have written and demonstrated that our natural abilities and characteristics are the same; that circumstances and educational opportunities not only shape or develop but also bestow upon a man his character as well as his particular mind and talents; that Alexander, in other circumstances, would have been a peace-loving Brahmin, Euclid—the author of sentimental novels, Attila—a tender shepherd, and Peter the Great—an ordinary man! If it should be necessary to refute this obvious falsity, then we could depict here a multitude of well-educated, learned people who possess everything but—feelings and reason. . . . No! Nature alone creates and bestows: education only shapes. Nature alone sows: art or moral instruction water the seed that it might flower better and more perfectly. The mind as well as the character of people is nature's concern: the father, the teacher, circumstances can help its subsequent development, but nothing more.—Whether nature connects our mental abilities and moral characteristics to certain special forms or activities of our physical being, we do not know: it is her secret. The system of Lavater and Doctor Gall seems to us now only a play of the imagination. The respected and wise Cabanis [1] himself, when he explained happiness and unhappiness in life by the characteristics of solids and fluids—temperament, passion, sorrow, and gaiety—did not undertake to measure and weigh as a pharmacist how much of what is necessary to produce a genius, a mathematician, a philosopher, a poet, a villain, or a virtuous man.

However this may be, in the world we see rational and emotional people, rational and cold, *from the cradle to the grave,* as the Russian proverb has it; and their moral characteristics are so independent of the will that all intellectual convictions, all firm intentions to change one's temperament, remain ineffectual. La Fontaine has said:

1. Johann Casper Lavater (1741–1801), a prominent Swiss phrenologist and mystic with whom Karamzin carried on a lengthy correspondence in the late eighties. Francis Joseph Gall (1758–1828), a German physician and one of the originators of phrenology. Pierre-Jean-Georges Cabanis (1758–1808), a French physician and author of *Rapports du physique et du moral de l'homme,* a study of the relation between the physiological and psychological sides of man.

> We are eternally that which we are predestined
> to be in the world.
> Chase nature out the door: It flies in the window! [2]

It is true that only the emotional know this bondage; the cold are always satisfied with themselves and do not wish to change. Does not such an observation alone indicate that advantages and happiness accrue to the latter? The former, undoubtedly, find keener delights; but since life has more woes than pleasures, then it is a boon to be less sensitive to one and the other. "The Gods do not bestow but sell us our pleasures," a Greek tragedian has said; "and much too dearly," it can be added, so that we with our purchases remain among the fools. But the emotional person is a natural wastrel: He sees his own ruin, struggles with himself, and buys everything.

However, in all fairness, let us point out also his natural superiorities. Impassive people usually are more prudent in everything, they live more humbly in this world, do less harm, and rarely disturb the harmony of society; but some emotional people make great sacrifices to virtue, astonish the world with their great deeds, in which, in Montaigne's words, "a little admixture of madness"—*un peu de folie*—is always neces-

2. This is probably a free rendition—or a quotation from a Russian translation—of La Fontaine's "La Chatte métamorphosée en femme," the last few lines of which are as follows:
En vain de son train ordinaire
On le veut désaccoutumer:
Quelque chose qu'on puisse faire,
On ne saurait le réformer.
Coups de fouche ni d'étrivières
Ne lui font changer de manières,
Et, fussiez-vous embâtonnés,
Jamais vous n'en serez les maîtres.
Qu'on lui ferme la porte au nez,
Il reviendra par les fenêtres.

sary; these people shine by the talent of their imagination and creative mind: poetry and eloquence are their gifts. Cold people can only be mathematicians, geographers, naturalists, antiquarians, and—if you will—philosophers!

We had the opportunity to become acquainted with the story of two individuals who represent in their persons these two characters.

Erast and Leonid were studying in the same pension and soon became friends. The first could be called handsome; the second attracted people's attention by his exceptionally intelligent face. A rare emotionalism was evident in the first from his very infancy; the second, apparently, was born prudent. Erast astonished people with his understanding, Leonid—with his diligence. Apparently, the first did not study but simply recalled the old; the second never forgot that which he had once learned. The first, postponing everything to the last minute because of an unwarranted self-assurance, sometimes did not learn his lesson; the second always knew it beforehand, continually went over it, and did not trust his memory. Erast sometimes committed little pranks, argued with his comrades, and frequently deserved punishment; but everyone loved him. Leonid behaved quietly, exemplarily, and offended no one; but he was only praised. One was considered sincere, good-natured: he actually was that. The other was suspected of being crafty, even deceitful: but he was only circumspect. —Their mutual friendship seemed a miracle: so dissimilar were their characters! But this friendship was based on that very difference of characteristics. Erast had the need of prudence, Leonid—the vivacity of ideas which for his soul had the *charm of the wonderful.* The emotionality of the one needed communication; the indifference and coldness of the other sought activity. Whan a man's heart and imagination are aflame, he loves to speak; when the soul is inactive, he listens with pleasure. Even in childhood Erast was captivated by novels, poetry, and most of all loved the extraordinary in history, examples of heroism and magnanimity. Leonid did not understand how one could be occupied by fantasies, that is, by novels! Poetizing seemed to him a difficult and useless play of the mind, and poetizers—people who want to run swiftly in fetters. He read history very diligently, but only to learn it, not for its intrinsic delight but as vocabulary or grammar. Is it any wonder that the opinions of these friends about its heroes were incompatible? Erast praised the magnanimity and courage of Alexander to the skies; Leonid called him a daring madman. The first said: "He conquered the universe!" The second answered: "And never knew why!" Erast revered Cato, the virtuous suicide; Leonid considered him insanely proud. Erast was delighted by the stormy periods of Greek and Roman freedom; Leonid thought that freedom was an evil when it did not allow people to live peacefully. Erast believed in everything extraordinary in history; Leonid doubted everything that did not conform to the normal order of things. One questioned with an ardent imagination, while the other—with his phlegmatic character.

As their opinions differed so did the actions of our friends. Once, the house in which they were studying and living caught fire at night: Erast leaped undressed from the bed, awoke Leonid and the other students; while putting out the fire, he saved the valuable things of his professor and never thought about his own. The house burned down and Erast, embracing his friend, said magnanimously, "I have lost everything; but in general calamities it is good to forget one's self. . . ."—"It is very bad," answered Leonid calmly; "man is created to think first of himself and then of others; otherwise the world could not exist. It is well that I was able to correct your thoughtlessness: I saved both the trunks and our books." Thus Leonid thought and acted in his sixteenth year.—Another time they were walking along the river bank: before their very eyes a boy fell from a bridge. Erast gasped and threw himself into the water. Leonid tried to restrain him but did not succeed; however, he did not lose his head, did not even cry out, but started running as quickly as possible toward some fishermen in the distance who were straightening out their nets—threw them a ruble and ordered them to save Erast, who was already drowning. The fishermen dragged him and the boy out in five minutes. Leonid castigated his friend: called him stupid, mad; however, he also wept. . . . The rare emotionality of cold people is all the more noticeable and touching. Erast kissed him and exclaimed: "I sacrificed myself to save a man, I am obligated for my life to my friend and I see his tears: what happiness!"

They left the pension at the same time and set off for the army together. Erast affirmed: "It is necessary to seek glory!" Leonid said: "Duty orders a nobleman to serve. . . ." The first rushed into danger—the other went where he was sent. The first, because of his easily inflamed temper, was quickly captured by the enemy; the other gained the name of a calm, prudent officer and the Cross of St. George at the end of the war. Peace freed Erast. . . . How sincerely he rejoiced in the promotion of his friend, who had far outstripped him in military rank. Not the slightest shadow of envy darkened his good, pure heart.—Together, they both transferred to the civil service. Leonid took a post that was difficult and not very brilliant; Erast entered the office of a very distinguished dignitary, hoping to gain his attention through his own talents and quickly to play a great role in the state. But for ambition to succeed, flexibility, constancy, coldness, patience are necessary; Erast certainly had none of these requisite characteristics. He wrote well; but, in submitting his document to the minister, he, haughtily, did not request condescending approbation but demanded due praise; he was not afraid to irritate him: he was

only afraid that he might demean himself before him. "Just so
he knows," said Erast to Leonid, "that I serve the state and not
him, and I agree to labor in obscurity for a long time so that I
might at some future date reach that rank which is worthy of a
noble ambition and in which my deeds will be famous in the
fatherland!" "Dear friend!' answered Leonid, "no talents can
promote a man in the state unless he satisfies people; if you do
not want to serve them, then they will not provide the means
for you to serve even the fatherland. Do not scorn the lower
rungs of the ladder: they lead to the top. A clever, ambitious
man only rarely glances at his distant goal but constantly
watches his immediate path so that he might move faithfully
toward it and not stumble. . . ." This slow, wise progression
could not satisfy the ardent Erast. Sometimes he worked with
amazing diligence; sometimes, exhausted by his labors, he
sought repose in worldly distractions. But this dangerous so-
called relaxation gradually became the major concern of his
life. Erast was young, handsome, intelligent, and rich: how
many reasons to enjoy the world! Women fawned upon him,
men envied him: How many pleasantries for one's heart and
self-esteem! He curtailed his evenings of work to prolong
them for the pleasures of society, finding that the approbatory
smile of a minister was not as attractive as the tender smile of
charming women. . . . In all due respect to him, we shall say
that he, having neglected his duties, was inwardly ashamed of
his failure; however, he would not endure the slightest rebukes and responded to them every time with a demand for
retirement. His minister was a good and reasonable man, but a
man; he lost his patience—and Erast finally became free, that
is, unemployed.

"Congratulate me on my dear liberty!" he said to Leonid,
running into his study.—"They have forbidden me to be
useful to the state: no one will forbid me to be happy." Leonid

shrugged his shoulders and coldly answered his friend: "I feel sorry for you! A twenty-five-year-old man should not be permitted to live for pleasure alone."

It should be understood that Erast, having retired, served the Graces all the more zealously. He was sincerely emotional: as a consequence, he wanted to love more than he wanted to be liked. Soon the enchantment of the tender passion presented the world to him in a single object and life in a single feeling. . . . The blissful lover, having forgot the universe, remembered only his friend and flew to him to speak of his own happiness.—The condescending Leonid put aside his official documents and listened to him; but often, leaning with his elbow on the fireplace, he dozed off amid the most vivacious descriptions of the new Saint-Preux, who in the fervor of his passionate eloquence sometimes did not notice him; and sometimes, startled by the soporific effect of his stories, which seemed extremely interesting to him, said plaintively, "You are dozing off! . . ." "My friend!" answered Leonid, "you lovers have the habit of repeating the same thing a hundred times; and every unnecessary repetition induces drowsiness in me." Leonid adhered to Buffon's system,[3] and spiritual love seemed to him a stupid fabrication of the human mind. Erast called him a coarse, unfeeling stone and other such endearing names. Leonid did not become angry, but maintained that a wise man had to occupy himself with business affairs in life and not with the playthings of an inflamed imagination.—The arguments of the friends continued—and were not resolved; but Erast sometimes abandoned his adored

3. Georges-Louis Leclerc de Buffon (1707–88), author of the voluminous *Histoire naturelle générale et particulière*, the "system" of which is based on the observation of phenomena, of reality, and then, on the basis of these observed and verifiable facts, the drawing of general conclusions.

beauty to go to Leonid and prove to him the indescribable happiness which a lover enjoys in the presence of his mistress! . . . Our cold-blooded philosopher smiled. . . .

He found still other opportunities to lord it over his opponent. Love for a long time has been compared to a rose, which captivates the sense of smell and the eyes but pricks the hand: unfortunately, the thorn outlasts the flower! . . . Erast, while enjoying the raptures, experienced the displeasures as well: sometimes he was bored, sometimes he bored others; sometimes he suffered from his own faithfulness, sometimes he was tortured by the inconstancy of his mistress. It should be noted that even the most brilliant young men for the most part enter liaisons with giddy women, who spare them an arduous chase: Is it any wonder that love and inconstancy mean about the same thing in this world? In tears, Erast sometimes threw himself into the embrace of his faithful friend to complain to him of the sweet deceivers. In such instances, Leonid acted magnanimously: he consoled and did not mock the poor sufferer. But honest Erast loved to blame himself, cursed the delusions of passions, wrote pungent satires on coquettes and at first read them only to his friend—and after several days to the women—and after several days tossed them in the fire, again captivated by some angel: because every languid charmer who took the trouble to assure him of her love usually seemed an ethereal being to him, and Leonid would have to fall asleep again while listening to the eloquent descriptions of her sweet characteristics and emotionality.—In a word, Erast was either blissfully happy or suffering torment, or, in the absence of real feelings, languishing in unendurable boredom. Leonid did not know happiness, but he did not seek it and was satisfied with the peaceful tranquillity of a soul lucid and gentle. The first revered freedom with his mind but with his heart always depended on other people; the second made his will conform to the order of things and did not know the burden of coercion. Erast *sometimes* envied Leonid's passiveness; Leonid *always* felt sorry for the ardent Erast.

The latter finally left P* in pursuit of a beauty—having abandoned Leonid, ill; on the way he became remorseful, believed he was disloyal to their friendship, wanted to turn back ten times, but, meanwhile, had already entered M—w, from which in a few days he informed his friend of his marriage. . . . "Convinced"—he wrote—"by many trials that all tender liaisons, based on pleasure alone, cannot endure, and that they leave, when broken, a heartfelt grief for the bygone delusion, I have resorted to a union sanctified by opinion and law! Its perpetuity captivates my soul, exhausted by inconstancy."—Erast beseeched his friend to hurry to his embrace and be a witness to his true happiness. Leonid soon appeared in M—w. . . . Erast, delighted, rushed to meet him, saying: "Now I see the proof of your tender friendship!"—"I requested leave," said Leonid calmly, "to go to my village. The road leads through M—w. . . ." And after two days he actually left.

Erast appeared happy to himself and to others: Nina, his spouse, was beautiful and sweet. He delighted both in the love and peace; but he soon observed in himself some strange inclination to melancholy: he grew pensive, despondent, and was glad when he was able to cry. The thought that his fate had been settled forever—that now he had nothing to desire in this world but must only fear loss—in some wondrous way disturbed his soul. We shall never explain this feeling to cold people: it will seem madness to them but it makes the happiest people unhappy. The imagination, which is not allowed by the ever busy heart to seek that mysterious beatitude beyond the distant horizon, is, as it were, wearied by its own inactivity and gives birth to the sad phantoms about us.

Leonid found Erast in this mood upon returning to M—w

from his village and promised to stay with him for a while. Nina desired to appear attractive to him. Is it any wonder? Erast had praised him so excessively! And the friends of husbands, as is known, have great claims on the attention of wives. Leonid, always impassive and calm, was therefore more interesting in society; his heart never prevented his mind from seeking at leisure pleasant conversational ideas. Furthermore, we have noted that cold people sometimes please women more than emotional ones. The latter, with excessive haste and without any *economy,* reveal themselves, while the former hide longer behind a shield of passivity and excite curiosity, which strongly affects a woman's imagination. There is a desire to see the phlegmatic heart in its ardent activity, there is a desire to animate the statue. . . . But without further elucidation, we shall say that Leonid suddenly—left for P*, bidding farewell neither to the master nor to the mistress.

Erast was dumfounded and hurried to his wife. Nina was bathed in tears, had written a letter and wanted to hide the paper from him. He tore the letter from her hands. . . . The poor husband but the happy friend! . . . It turned out that Nina adored Leonid but that he did not want to betray the friendship and had withdrawn for this reason. In the letter the injudicious woman implored him to return and threatened to poison herself if he did not. . . . Erast was numb with fear. . . . His guilty spouse lay senseless at his feet. . . . Seeing her deadly pallor, he forgot everything and tried only to bring her back to consciousness. . . . Nina opened her languid eyes. I do not know what she said to Erast, but after several minutes, Erast, having pressed her to his heart, loudly exclaimed: "Such angelic repentance is sweeter than chastity itself; I have forgotten everything and we shall be happy!" That very day he wrote to Leonid: "O friend, faithful and priceless! Your action eclipses Scipio's virtue; but I venture to believe that in similar circumstances, I would have done the same!" Leonid, in his reply, expressed regret at *his domestic difficulties* and said, in passing: "Women are lovable and weak, like children; much must be forgiven them; but what reasonable man would sacrifice an old friend to their passing caprice?"

Tender hearts are always ready to forgive magnanimously and they are delighted by the thought that they thus acquire new claims on the love of the guilty, but the repentance of a weak soul does not strengthen its virtuous feelings for long: like the quivering musical string, it gradually grows still and the soul again assumes that disposition which leads to vice. It is easier to restrain oneself from the first fault than from the second—and poor Erast divorced his wife, since not all his acquaintances, like Leonid, saved themselves by fleeing from the charms of Nina.

We see unhappy husbands in our world and have almost grown accustomed to them, but if they are emotional, then may one not sincerely pity them? We love to weep with a grieving widower; he is happy when compared with a husband who must hate or despise his spouse! Erast in his despair complained of his fate but more—of women. "I loved you fervently and tenderly," he said, "I could be constant to the most fickle women, I could be honorable in the most immoral liaison, I saw how you forgot your duties but I remembered my own—and this is my reward; having been deserted several times, I have finally become a cuckold!" Erast wept for some two weeks, wandered for some two weeks alone through the environs of the town, and there, wanting to busy himself with something or other, decided to become—an author.

The emotional heart is a rich source of ideas: if reason and taste assist it, then success is undoubted and fame awaits the writer. Erast lived in solitude, but soon attracted general attention; the intelligent pronounced his name with respect, and the good—with love, because he was born a tender friend of humanity and in his creations depicted a soul passionately interested in the welfare of people. The apparition, called glory, appeared to him in her glittering radiance and inflamed him with a burning desire for immortality. "O Glory!" he thought, enraptured.—"I sought you once in the smoke of battle and on the bloodstained field; today, in my quiet study, I see your brilliant image before me and dedicate the remainder of my life to you. I could not be happy, but I can be the object of wonder; garlands of myrtle fade with youth; the garland of laurel grows green even on the grave! . . ." Poor Erast! You have exchanged one daydream for another. Glory is beneficial to the world but not to those who acquire it! Soon the vipers of envy began to hiss, and the good-natured author acquired enemies. These queer people, whom he did not know personally, grew pale and suffered at his authorial successes; they wrote vile, venomous lampoons and were ready to tear the man apart who had offended them neither in deed nor in thought. Erast vainly challenged the covetous to write better than he: they were only able to pour out their poison and bile and were not distinguished by talent. Erast was weak enough to be vexed by their hatred and wrote to his friend: "Having discovered the fickleness of women, I now see the rancor of men. At least the former can be excused as an amusement: the latter commit evil without any profit to themselves." "Surest of all," Leonid answered, "is to make one's way in the world by the main road and to store up money which is accepted everywhere. Service is our surest path to respect (which people in a civil union naturally seek) while rank—the current coin; let us suppose that glory is more valuable, but do many know its stamp and high standard? It is not a coin but a medal: only an expert will accept it in place of money. Furthermore, the gifts of the mind are always disputable and the reason is obvious: petty but proud souls, of which there are enough in this world, want to elevate themselves by demeaning the great. But the deed is done, and you stand on the path of glory: Be firm enough to scorn the efforts of envy, an unavoidable obligation of a famous name. Don't only scorn but be pleased by it, because it proves that you are famous." Leonid's letter concluded with these words: "I shall marry in a month so that I may be relieved of household cares. A woman is necessary for order in the home."

Erast forgot his authorial vexations to hurry to the wedding of his friend in P*. . . . They had not seen each other for a long time. Leonid, despite the strenuous activity of a busy man, was a picture of health; because every dietetic rule begins with the prescription: "Be spiritually calm!" Erast, at one time a handsome young man, had grown thin as a skeleton; because "the fiery passions," according to the words of one Englishman, "are the couriers of life: traveling with them, it is not far to the grave." Love and glory feed the soul but not the body. Leonid, despite his coldness, noted Erast's pallor with great pity. . . . He had not deceived his friend and had actually married only "for order in the home," having beforehand stipulated to his betrothed that she: "(1) go visiting once a week; (2) receive guests once a week; (3) enter his study once a day and only for five minutes." She, carrying out the will of her father, agreed to everything and strictly observed the prescriptions of her husband, the more willingly since the melancholic Erast, who was living in their home, loved to sit with her by the fireplace and read French novels to her. Sometimes they wept together, like children, and soon their souls in some wondrous way grew attuned to each other. The first stirring of sympathy necessitated frankness: in such a situation the heart has all the perspicacity of penetrating reason and knows that sincerity is more powerful than the most eloquent assurances of friendship. Callista found out details of Erast's life which were unknown to her husband—and it is amazing: she listened to Erast with a most vivacious pleasure, while Leonid listened coldly. Repaying trust with trust, Callista complained to him of Leonid's indifference and said once: "I would like to have known that foolish Nina, in order to understand a woman who could not be happy with you!" But even without words she made herself clear to Erast. Sympathetic emotionality has its own language, before which all others must yield in expressiveness; and if, in general, the eyes serve as a mirror of the soul, then what cannot a passionate woman express with them? Callista's every action showed every minute that Erast had—to withdraw! He wanted to deceive himself but could not; he was terrified of being loved, but did not cease being lovable; he wanted to part forever, but saw Callista from morning until evening. What did the wise Leonid do, while this was going on? He was busy with his office affairs. Cold people are not blind, however—and one morning poor Erast was told that he was the master of Leonid's home! That is, without further ado, our phlegmatic sat his wife in the carriage and successfully left P* with her, having written the following note to his friend: "You will be an eternal child, but Callista is a woman. I know you and want to save you from the reproaches of your conscience. I have been commissioned to conclude an important state affair a thousand versts from here. Your friend—faithful unto the grave. . . ." The readers can be merciful to Erast: the gnawings of his conscience punished him sufficiently. For the tender heart any conceivable disaster amounts to nothing when compared with a situation in which it must reproach itself. "Foolish man!" he thought. "I have tempted the wife of a friend, who would not take advantage of the frailty of my wife! This is the reward for his virtue! Oh shame! I dared not to be affected by her and thought that I, myself, would be able to act in the same way [as my friend]! . . ." We must say to Erast's honor that he was not annoyed at Leonid for leaving with Callista.

Fate sent consolation. He found out that Leonid's father-in-

law was involved in an important lawsuit and, in all probability, would lose his estate. Secretly, Erast sent a large draft in
his own name to the other litigant on the condition that he
call off the suit. This magnanimous sacrifice was all the more
pleasing to him since both Leonid and Callista were the
recipients; he did not want to love but he allowed himself to
pity the weak woman, who had forgotten her duty *for him!*

Erast sought distraction in travel, which is fascinating in
those years when the world is still new to the heart; when we,
in the enchantment of hope, are still preparing to live, to act
rationally, and to enjoy our emotionality; when in a word we
want to store up pleasant recollections for the future and the
means to please people. But the soul, exhausted by passion—
the soul, which has tasted all the sweetness and bitterness of
life—can it still be curious? What can it still learn, when it
has known through experience the raptures and tortures of
love, the charm of glory and its inner emptiness? Erast had
not the *pleasure of envying* people because his heart no longer
wished to believe in happiness. Looking at majestic palaces, he
thought: "Here they weep just as in the cottage,"—entering
the temples of learning, he said to himself: "Here they teach
everything except how to find well-being in life,"—looking at
a handsome youth, happy in the tender smiles of some charm-
ers, he thought: "You will pay for your victories." Erast imagined that his heart finally had become inured: emotional people, those who have suffered enough grief, always think in this
way; but upon hearing some soft music, he forgot himself, and
his chest was dampened by tears; seeing a poor man, he
wanted to help him, and, when his eyes met the glance of
some pretty stranger, he sought, *unbeknown* to himself, an
affectionate response. Erast sometimes wrote and inwardly
consoled himself with the thought that envy and enmity die
with the author and that his creations would find in posterity
only justice and recognition; as a consequence, he still con-

stantly deceived himself with his imagination. Do not cold souls astonish us with their fervor when they mutilate the memory of poor Jean-Jacques? Slander is an inherited sin of people: the living and the dead are equally its object.

Erast returned to his fatherland so that he might not leave his bones in an alien land: because his health was poor. He burned with impatience to see his friend but he remembered his guilt and he feared his glance. Leonid, already a distinguished personage in the state, was really glad to see him and introduced a young beauty, his second wife. Callista had already quit this world: her consort, not having removed his mourning clothes as yet, had become engaged to another and *exactly* a year later had wed. Erast did not dare to weep in the presence of Leonid but grieved spiritually: Callista was the last object of his tender weakness! His friend treated him kindly but did not offer to allow him to live in his home!

Erast intended to devote the remainder of his life to a quiet seclusion and literature, but, unfortunately, he was given a medallion with locks of Callista's hair and a letter which she had written to him six days before her demise. He realized that Callista had loved him passionately, he realized that this love, so contrary to the demands of virtue, had shortened her life. Poor Erast! His melancholy turned into despair. Ah! It is a hundred times better to be deceived by unfaithful mistresses than to destroy a faithful one! In the delirium of grief, he visited Callista's grave every day to shed tears and he lacerated himself with reproaches; however, there were also minutes during which Erast secretly enjoyed the thought that he, if but once in his life, had been loved fervently! . . .

He soon fell ill, but managed still to transfer half his estate to Nina when he discovered that she suffered from want. This woman, punished by fate for her unfaithfulness and deeply moved by the generosity of her spouse, whom she had offended, hurried to fall at his feet. Erast died in her arms, uttering the names of Callista and Nina with love: *His soul had been reconciled to women but not to fate!* . . . Leonid did not visit the patient because the doctors had termed his illness infectious; he also did not attend the burial, saying: "That soulless body is not my friend! . . ." Two people buried him and wept with sincere grief: Nina and Erast's kind valet.

Leonid lived to a ripe old age, enjoying distinction, wealth, health, and tranquillity. The sovereign and the sovereignty valued his service, intelligence, industry, and integrity, but no one, except Erast, had been sincerely devoted to him. He did much good but without any inner pleasure and only for his own security; he did not respect people but was cautious with them; he did not seek pleasures but he avoided vexations; an *absence of suffering* seemed a delight, and indifference—the talisman of wisdom. If we could believe in the transmigration of souls, then we would have to conclude that his soul had suffered a great deal in its original condition and wanted only to rest in the body of Leonid. He lost his spouse and children but, realizing the uselessness of grief, tried to forget them.— His favorite thought was that everything in this world served man, and man served only himself. At the end of his life Leonid would have agreed to live it over, but he did not desire this: because he was ashamed to desire the impossible. He died without hope or fear just as, generally, he dropped off to sleep in the evening.

1803